Racso and the Rats of NIMH

Sequel to Robert C. O'Brien's

Mrs. Frisby and the Rats of NIMH

Jane Leslie Conly

illustrations by Leonard Lubin

■ HarperCollins*Publishers*

Racso and the Rats of NIMH
Text copyright © 1986 by Jane Leslie Conly
Illustrations copyright © 1986 by Leonard B. Lubin
All rights reserved. No part of this book may be
used or reproduced in any manner whatsoever
without written permission except in the case of
brief quotations embodied in critical articles and
reviews. Printed in the United States of America.
For information address HarperCollins Children's
Books, a division of HarperCollins Publishers,
10 East 53rd Street, New York, NY 10022.
Designed by Al Cetta

Library of Congress Cataloging-in-Publication Data
Conly, Jane Leslie.
  Racso and the rats of NIMH.
  Sequel to: Mrs. Frisby and the rats of NIMH /
Robert C. O'Brien.
  Summary: Timothy Frisby, a field mouse, teams up
with the adventurous young rat Racso as together they
try to prevent the destruction of a secret community
of rats that can read and write.
  [1. Mice—Fiction. 2. Rats—Fiction] I. Lubin,
Leonard B., ill.   II. O'Brien, Robert C. Mrs. Frisby
and the rats of NIMH.   III. Title.
PZ7.C761844Ras 1986   [Fic]   85-42634
ISBN 0-06-021361-2
ISBN 0-06-021362-0 (lib. bdg.)

10   11   12   13   14   15   16   17   18   19   20

for Eliza

Contents

Racso and the Rats of NIMH

Emergency!

Mrs. Frisby, a brown field mouse, hummed softly to herself as she folded her son Timothy's clothing: a sweater, a jacket, a red scarf. The latter needed mending, she noted, and set it in a separate pile from the others. It was unusual for her to be alone in the house, as she was now. Her children, Martin, Cynthia, Teresa, and Timothy, were harvesting today. There was a great deal to be done. Over the summer Martin, her elder son, had found a mate, a lovely young mouse named Breta. They had moved to a small nest under a rotted sycamore stump in the meadow. Now food for the winter must be gathered for his family, too. And tomorrow Timothy would leave home to go to school. This would be his third year as a student in a school run by the superintelligent Rats of Nimh.

He had learned a great deal there—so much that Mrs. Frisby had lost track of the subjects he had studied. He could read and write, did math problems, and knew that the earth was round, which was hard for Mrs. Frisby to believe. He knew the constellations and could predict with a good deal of accuracy how long it would take to travel to a place where one had never been before. Thinking of travel made Mrs. Frisby sigh. For the school was a long way off—miles and miles away, in a remote section of the state forest called Thorn Valley. It was so far that Timothy was not able to come home during the school session, which lasted for nine months of the year. Mrs. Frisby missed him terribly.

So I must mend his scarf, she thought, and I will pack his favorite foods in his knapsack, in case he doesn't reach Thorn Valley in time for dinner tomorrow. And I must clean out the cupboard, to make room for the beans that the children will be bringing. With that thought she hurried into her kitchen, which was really one half of a cinder block mired deep in the earth near a large stone in the Fitzgibbons' garden. Mrs. Frisby loved the cinder-block house: It was cozy and warm in winter, and it was *safe*—ever since the rats had moved it out of the path of Mr. Fitzgibbon's plow. For an instant Mrs. Frisby recalled that terrible spring three years ago, when Timothy had been sick with pneumonia and the cinder-block house in danger of being crushed in the March plowing. The rats had worked all night, moving the house into the lee of the stone, where the dirt remained unturned throughout the year. Mrs. Frisby still felt a debt of gratitude to the rats for saving her house and her son's life.

Today the sunlight fell through the entrance hole into her kitchen in a lovely golden arc. Mrs. Frisby stood in it for a moment, feeling it warm her head and back. Then she reached for a broom and began to sweep some bits of corn husk into a pile. She had almost finished doing this when she heard—from someplace up above her head—a great to-do.

"Mrs. MOUSE!" rasped a loud voice. "TIMO-THY'S MOTHER, come OUT!"

Mrs. Frisby hurried up the entrance hole, broom in hand, and poked her head out cautiously to see who was there. It was young Jeremy, a crow she had once befriended, and he was hopping up and down in agitation.

"Mrs. FRISBY!" he shouted. "I was so upset I forgot your name!"

"Goodness, Jeremy," Mrs. Frisby said, "Calm down. And tell me what's wrong."

"I can't take Timothy to school tomorrow!" Jeremy shouted. He looked close to tears. "It's an EMERGENCY! I have to go home right away. My mother is very sick. She flew into a ladder and broke her wing." And with that a large tear slid down the black feathers under Jeremy's eye.

"Now, now," Mrs. Frisby said, keeping her voice calm for Jeremy's benefit.

"My cousin brought the news this morning," Jeremy added. "I went to Mr. Ages and he says that she may not fly for a whole month. And he gave me some powder for her to swallow after dinner."

Secretly Mrs. Frisby was surprised that Jeremy had thought to visit Mr. Ages, the white mouse who served as doctor for the wild animals who lived on the farm. "You did well," she said. "And, of course, you should fly home. Your mother will need your help."

"But what about Timothy? School starts next week,

and I was supposed to fly him to Thorn Valley tomorrow!"

"We will manage," Mrs. Frisby said, although inside she wondered *how* they would manage. "You must stay with your mother while she needs you."

"Will she die?" Jeremy asked. Another tear slid through his black feathers.

"Of course not!" Mrs. Frisby said, but when she saw Jeremy's stricken expression she tried to make her tone more kindly. "Just make sure she takes Mr. Ages's powder. Within a month her wing should be as good as new."

"Thank you!" Jeremy said. "Oh, thank you!"

"You're welcome," Mrs. Frisby said dryly, and she ducked her head to avoid the flap of Jeremy's large wings as he heaved himself into the air.

"SEE YOU LATER!" he shrieked from up above her—loud enough to be heard for a mile around, she thought to herself—and then he quickly flew away.

Mrs. Frisby retrieved her broom and returned slowly to her kitchen. She sat down in the corner of the room and tried to think. She knew that going to school was the most important thing that had ever happened to Timothy, and that he must continue.

He was not a strong mouse and never would be physically strong, so it was all the more important that he have an education. Then when trouble did come along—for surely everyone must anticipate at least a small amount of misfortune—he would be able to reason his way out of it. Timothy knew the way to Thorn Valley—he had seen the route four times from up on Jeremy's back as they flew over the woods—but he had never made such a long trip on foot. And this year there was no one who could go with him.

"Of course I can do it, Mother," he said, as they sat eating the ripe kidney beans the children had brought home. "I know exactly how the river winds and where the trail goes north. The trip from there will only be one day."

"But the whole trip will take four days," Mrs. Frisby said.

"I'd get there the day before school starts," Timothy said. "That is, if I leave tomorrow."

"What about food? I'm not sure you can carry a four-day supply."

"I won't have to carry that much," Timothy said eagerly. "The autumn olives are out everywhere—we had some for lunch today. And the acorns will be at their best. I do love fresh acorns."

Mrs. Frisby looked at her small son. His eyes were bright with excitement. "I know how much you want to go," she said, "but I'm not promising anything. I'll think about it while you sleep."

Timothy nodded, but he was unusually quiet during the rest of the meal, and several times he smiled to himself. Mrs. Frisby could tell that he was thinking about the trip.

Later in the night, as she sat alone in the kitchen, Martin came to talk to his mother.

"I think you should let Timothy go," he said. "He's starting to grow up. Today he picked more beans than any of us. And school means so much to him."

"I know that," Mrs. Frisby said, "but it's a long journey, with many dangers. And Timothy has never traveled alone."

"I wish I could go with him," Martin said, "but I don't want to leave Breta for so long, and I still have more harvesting to do."

"Of course," Mrs. Frisby said. She kissed her son good night, and after he left she thought of her husband, Jonathan, who had died four years ago. He had been on a mission for the rats when he had died.

"No gains without a risk," he had often told her. Yet losing him made her want to keep the children wih her for a long, long time.

Mrs. Frisby sat thinking until very late. By the time she went to bed the moon had moved from above the field to behind the trees, and the owl had returned from his nightly hunt. She fell asleep with her mind made up.

The Journey

The morning was crisp and clear. Mrs. Frisby was up early, preparing breakfast. When the three children emerged from their bed of straw and fluff, she looked Timothy squarely in the face and said, "You may go."

For the next hour Timothy made and discarded lists of what to take in his knapsack. A jacket for winter, the scarf, a small pocketknife (a gift from the rats on his completion of last year's term), some dried beans, a portion of sweetened oats from the bin in the Fitzgibbons' barn. A pocket dictionary. A pencil. A piece of string.

[9]

"Why?" Mrs. Frisby asked.

"To make a splint, in case I should break my leg," Timothy said.

Mrs. Frisby decided not to ask any more questions.

Timothy also drew a map on a scrap of paper and gave it to his mother. He showed her a wiggly line, which was meant to be the river, and another line, which lay close and then moved farther away from the first—the trail. "Thorn Valley is here," he said, pointing to the top part of the paper, "in case you need me, or decide to come and visit." Mrs. Frisby was not sure that those lines would help her find a place beyond the river and across a high mountain; but she folded the paper neatly and put it in a small hole where she kept a few valued possessions.

Finally he was ready to leave. Martin, Teresa, and Cynthia agreed to walk with Timothy across the meadow to the edge of the woods, but Mrs. Frisby kissed her son good-bye at the edge of the entrance hole. "The rats will be good to you," she said. "Please send word of how you are, Timothy. And don't travel at night." She smiled. "We will miss you."

The Journey

*   *   *

And so Timothy began his journey.

He waved good-bye to his sisters and brother at the border of the forest and walked northeast, keeping low to the ground as he had been taught. The fallen leaves, which rustled in the breeze, were an excellent camouflage and made Timothy's slight movements almost unnoticeable. He had tucked a beech leaf over the bulk of his knapsack, so that it would not be visible. He felt extremely happy.

He walked for several hours without stopping. Eventually he came to a stream. The sun was directly overhead, and he was beginning to feel a bit tired. He sat down under a small bush and rested, and let his hind feet float in the water. He removed the beech leaf and took off his knapsack, but rather than eat any of his provisions, he found a broken walnut on the ground not far from where he had been resting. In the twisted cavities there were several nut meats that a larger animal had been unable to reach. His small paws removed them easily, and they were wonderfully sweet. Along the streambed he saw salamanders and crayfish creeping among the rocks, and he watched them until he felt rested and ready to go on.

He followed the stream as it wound slowly north-
ward. The woods were very still. Twice he heard
the hammering of a woodpecker, each time from a
distance away, and he thought once he heard crows
calling. He took cover then, for their cry is often a
warning of hawks or owls. But the sound faded, and
he continued on his way.

About a half mile above the spot where he had
stopped to rest, Timothy began to notice something
puzzling. Here and there along the trail the leaves
were pushed aside, as if some animal had recently,
and very carelessly, followed the same path. Timothy knew that no wild animal would leave such a
noticeable trail. Perhaps, he thought, it is only the
wind, which blows stronger along the banks of the
stream where there are no trees. Yet each time he
began to think that the wind was the cause, he would
come across a place that seemed a little too messy.

As the sun began to slant through the trees from
the west, he decided to find a place to sleep. Only
a short distance up the path he saw a small oak tree
with a knothole in it. He scurried up the trunk until
he was just below the hole. Cautiously, he looked
inside. There was a small room, clean and dry! It
was perfect. Timothy stashed the knapsack in one

corner, then scouted the area and spotted a clump
of wild mushrooms growing on a rotting elm stump.
Dinner! He pulled up two mushrooms and carried
them up the tree into the hollow space. He ate as
much as he wanted and then spread his jacket on
the rough floor. The sun had sunk below the tree
line, so it was now almost completely dark. He lay
down and went to sleep.

He woke only once in the night. He was dreaming, and in his dream he had finished school at Thorn
Valley and was now an engineer. He decided to
build his family a beautiful house, a house such as
no field mouse had ever lived in. He designed it out
of stone, with many rooms and an open space for
picnics or napping in the center of the house. He
was in his bedroom, reading, and could hear the
murmur of his sisters' voices in the open court. He
sensed vaguely that there was something wrong in
his design, and that they were in danger. Suddenly
a scream split the air. HAWK! He woke up, shaking.
Peeping out of the knothole, he saw that the woods
were bathed in moonlight, so that each tree cast a
faint shadow on the ground. In his own tree, where
the lower branches were outlined among the fallen
leaves, was the silhouette of a huge bird. He crept

back to bed and pushed his jacket into the farthest corner of the hollow space. He curled into a tiny ball and hid his face. After a while he went back to sleep.

When he woke up, sunlight was streaming into his room. He looked out cautiously, and up; the hawk was gone. He ate more mushroom and treated himself to a bit of the oats his mother had packed for him. Then he slid down the tree trunk and was on his way.

It was another beautiful day. Timothy drank from the stream. Humming a tune to match the rippling of the water, he skipped along the path. The leaves gave off a lovely musky smell. He trotted along happily, and then stopped short.

Ahead of him in the trail were the remains of a tiny campfire. The wood was still smoldering and several of the burning sticks had twigs that stretched out into the fallen leaves. It was clear that the fire could spread! Timothy rushed to the spot, broke the twigs off, and threw them into the middle of the fire. He climbed down into the streambed and carried several loads of pebbles and wet sand back up the bank and dumped them on the fire. It steamed and hissed. He folded a large leaf into a shallow cup and carried water up the bank to pour onto the smoldering heap. Finally he was certain that the fire was completely out.

Timothy was astounded. He could not imagine who would build such a fire and then forget to put it out! Yet it was clear that the fire had been built by a small animal, one that was just his size, or perhaps a little bigger.

He continued along the trail. Now he was cautious; he realized that he was traveling not far behind an animal that was different from any he had ever known. Perhaps it was dangerous, even fierce. He took cover every few feet and stopped to listen. He noticed that the leaves along the trail continued to be pushed aside, as if someone had plowed his way right down the middle, without the least concern for covering his trail. Once he noticed a shred of paper on the trail. He stopped and picked it up. It was brown, with writing on it; he could decipher

HERSH
MINIA
CHOC

The paper had a strong sweet smell.

The sun was high in the sky. Timothy felt quite

hot and had just made the decision to sit down and rest under a bush when he heard a voice from the direction of the stream. It was crying, "HELP! HELP! HELP!"

A New Friend

Timothy stopped stock-still. A wave of fear swept through him as the shouts continued. Suddenly he felt small and very young. He might be hurt or even killed trying to save this unknown animal. On the other hand, he was the only one around to help. He hurried to the stream bank and peeked over the side.

A very small rat was floating in a whirlpool upstream, clinging desperately to a stick with its front paws. The water was deep and fast flowing. Timothy could not see its face. It struggled pitifully and shouted again, "HELP!"

Timothy broke off a thin sapling and dragged it

down the bank to the water's edge just opposite the rat. He flung off his knapsack and, bracing himself behind a stone, extended the branch as far as it would reach, almost to the center of the stream. "Here!" he yelled. "Grab this!"

The rat spun around, saw the branch, and lunged for it. It sank completely under the water, but within seconds it emerged and grasped the branch with both paws. Only its nose was above the waterline, and it was a dead weight in the stream. Timothy pulled the branch in hand over hand for as long as he could, then angled it downstream so that the rat would be swept into a shallow channel about half a foot from the shore. Within seconds it was there, a gray, wet heap against the rocky streambed.

The rat lay still for a long time, so long that Timothy began to think that it might have died. Then he heard it choking, a rasping series of coughs. Again it lay still, then it groaned, got up on all four legs, and shook itself. It turned around and saw Timothy.

"You . . ." it said. "*You* saved me."

Timothy nodded.

"Saved by a mouse," the rat muttered. "Wait till my family hears about this."

Timothy had never seen such a small rat, but he

decided to keep that observation to himself. "My name is Timothy Frisby," he said.

"I'm Racso," said the rat. "How do you do?"

Racso rested and dried himself on a stone in the sunshine. He did not look at Timothy or speak to him. After a while he got up and searched among the leaves until he uncovered a paper bag. He reached inside it and took out a black beret, and jammed it on his head. He shot Timothy a suspicious glance and checked the contents of the bag. Satisfied, he nodded to himself and tucked the bag under his arm.

Timothy could not decide whether to stay or go. He was very curious about the rat: who he was, where he had come from, why he was so small. On the other hand, Racso did not seem inclined to talk. And he had not been particularly appreciative about the rescue. In fact, he seemed to think he was somehow superior to Timothy. Timothy knew that if he delayed too long he would not arrive in time for the first day of school.

"It was nice to meet you," he told the rat.

"Quite," said the rat.

"Good-bye," Timothy said.

"Good-bye," said Racso.

Timothy put on his knapsack, but as he began to

walk down the path he heard the rat get up and begin to follow him. He looked around. Sure enough, Racso was walking about twenty feet behind him, scattering leaves in every direction. Timothy stopped. "Since you're going my way," he told the rat, "I'll wait and walk with you."

They walked together for some time without speaking. As Racso's fur dried, Timothy noticed that he was really quite an attractive rat, despite his small stature. He had a jaunty, self-confident gait and occasionally whipped his tail smartly through the air, tossing the leaves up behind him in a small cloud. Sometimes he sang a song under his breath, with lyrics and music Timothy had never heard before: "Gonna find my bay-bee, gonna take her home with me."

They walked for several hours. Timothy could see that Racso was getting tired. Finally the rat said, "I've got to stop and rest."

Timothy pointed to a flat stone under a shade tree.

"Good," said Racso, and then, "Have you eaten?"

"Not since breakfast."

"I've got something good to eat." He opened the paper bag and dug around inside with his paw. "Here." He handed Timothy something in a brown wrapper. Timothy saw that the paper was identical to the shredded paper he had found on the trail earlier.

"What is it?"

Racso looked astounded. "It's candy."

"What is candy?"

"What is CANDY? I didn't think there was anyone on earth who didn't know what candy is!"

"I didn't think there was anyone on earth who would go into a stream if he couldn't swim," Timothy answered.

The rat's eyes met his briefly. "Here," he said, taking the object back into his paws. He tore off the paper, uncovering a brown molded thing. He broke off a piece of it and gave it to Timothy. "Eat it."

Timothy tasted the brown stuff and was overpowered with its sweet, waxy flavor. "It's wonderful!" he said.

"You may have the whole bar," said Racso. "I brought an entire bag with me. They've been quite heavy to carry, but there aren't many left now."

Timothy felt a little self-conscious as he unwrapped his own corn-husk packets. "Would you like a kidney bean?" he asked.

Racso made a face. "Where did you get it?"

"I picked them in Mr. Fitzgibbon's field."

"Oh," said Racso, with a look of superior understanding. "Then you must be a *field mouse.*"

"Correct," Timothy said shortly.

"I'm not a field rat," said Racso. "I'm a city rat. I left my family and all my girlfriends. They cried, of course, and they pleaded, but I told them I had to go. I'm in pursuit of a better life. I have friends here in the country, rats who can read and write." Racso looked at Timothy to see whether he was impressed, but Timothy regarded him levelly.

"What are the rats' names?" he asked carefully.

Racso looked a little embarrassed. "Actually, I don't know their names," he said. "But I know they live somewhere in this direction."

"Have you met them before?"

"Actually, no," Racso said. "But I'm sure they will be glad to meet ME."

"How will you find them?"

"I'll keep walking in this direction, then I'll turn and follow the trail north where the river splits," Racso said. "If what my old man says is right, it'll be about one day's trip from there."

"So your father is a friend of theirs?"

"He was," Racso said. Timothy thought he seemed to hesitate, as if he weren't sure whether to tell the whole story. But then he went on. "He once shared a cage with one of them, at a laboratory called Nimh.

Scientists taught them how to read, and gave them special shots to make them smart. They got so smart that they figured out how to escape. My dad lived with them for a while. They had a big nest with electric lights and running water and a big refrigerator! But there was a fight, and my dad and some of the other rats left."

"What happened then?"

"I don't know everything. All I know is that my old man was in an accident so bad that the rest of his friends were killed. He was burned, but he managed to save himself. After he got better, he went back to the city instead of the colony. He found my mom and moved back in with her. And after that my sister and I were born."

An idea about who Racso's father was had begun to grow in Timothy's mind, but before he could ask more questions Racso spoke again. This time it was as if he were arguing with someone who wasn't there.

"Learning is important!" he said. "I've got to educate myself. I can't spend my whole life lying around in the sewers eating garbage."

"Have you been to school?"

Racso shook his head sadly. "There are no schools for rats in the city. My dad taught me a few things, but then he got scared. He said education had almost killed him, and it had killed six other rats. He said those shots the humans gave him had turned him into a misfit. He said if there's one thing I need to remember, it's that I'm a rat, and nothing more."

"How did you convince him to let you come here?"

"I didn't. I ran away." Racso grinned, but there was a hint of nervousness in his voice. "I'm on my own now. I'm going to get my education and become a scientist. I'm going to make discoveries and become famous. I'll be on TV and on the cover of *Time* magazine."

"But how did you know where to go?"

"My dad had the accident in a town called Smithville, so I asked different animals and birds which highway went toward it, and they told me. It turned out there were big green signs along the highway, but I couldn't read them. I bribed a squirrel to lead me into town—I gave him three candy bars—" Racso shook his head sadly—"and the local rats knew how to get to Mr. Fitzgibbon's farm. Then I met this dumb crow who told me how to get to Thorn Valley. I offered him candy, but all he wanted was a silver cigarette paper I'd pulled out of the trash that morning."

Timothy stiffened. "What was the crow's name?"

"Oh, I don't know, Jimmy or Jerry or something like that. He was all shook up because his mother was sick, and he wanted the silver paper for a present for her." Racso shook his head. "What a jerk!"

"His name is Jeremy," Timothy said coldly. "He may not be the smartest bird in the world, but he's kindhearted, and he would have given you the directions for nothing. You didn't have to bribe him."

"My old man taught me that nobody gets something for nothing."

"Your old man . . ." Timothy was certain now that he knew who Racso's father was. In the written history of the rats' adventures, there was a whole chapter devoted to him. It was called "Jenner's Tragedy."

They sat for a moment in silence. Timothy was fascinated by the situation he found himself in. He, like the rats, had assumed that Jenner was dead. Not only was he alive, but he had a son, and his son had a lot in common with Timothy. Both their fathers had escaped from Nimh, and both sons had left home to get an education. Still, Racso's superior attitude was irritating. Timothy decided to teach him a lesson. He deliberately kept his expression casual as he reached into his knapsack and pulled out the little dictionary. He cleared his throat and turned the pages until he came to the one he was looking for.

[25]

"RAT," he read aloud, "R-A-T. Any of certain rodents (genus *Rattus*, and allied genera) distinguished from mice by their larger size and differences in teeth. The best-known species are the brown, or Norway, rat, the black rat, and the roof rat. . . .''

Racso's eyes opened wide in disbelief. He opened his mouth to speak, but nothing came out.

Timothy continued. "MOUSE . . . any of numerous species of small rodents, especially the house mouse, found in human habitations throughout the world; compare VOLE."

"You . . ." Racso squeaked, "you . . . you . . . you . . ."

Timothy smiled.

"YOU CAN READ!" Racso shouted.

Timothy nodded.

"Will you teach me? Please?"

Timothy was silent. Racso groaned. "I'll give you anything you want if only you'll teach me, Timothy."

Timothy smiled slightly, but he shook his head. Racso looked ready to burst into tears.

"I won't teach you," Timothy said. "But I have friends who will. Rat friends. They have a school at Thorn Valley, and they teach almost every subject you can name: reading, writing, carpentry, math, astronomy . . ."

"The rats of Nimh," Racso whispered reverently.

Timothy nodded. "I'm on my way to school right now," he said. "And you may come with me."

A Narrow Escape

It was almost an hour before Racso let Timothy put the dictionary away, so that they could resume walking. "Just one more word," he would plead; or he would ask, "Is this the letter B?" Finally Timothy began to feel concerned about the time.

"We've got to move on," he said. "It's only a few hours until twilight, and we'll have to stop then."

They hurried down the trail. In another hour they began to hear the sound of the river to the west, and several times Timothy thought he could see the gleam of the river through the brush. They agreed to camp where the stream and the river merged. A brisk wind tossed the leaves up in their faces, and they arrived at the juncture just as the sunlight was beginning to fade. "I'll make a campfire," said Racso, but Timothy pointed out a large bird's nest in the middle branches of a birch tree. It was tattered and had clearly been abandoned for several seasons.

"It's perfect," he said. "The high edges will shelter us from the wind, and it's probably lined with feathers, too. Anyway, it would be dangerous to make a fire on such a windy day." They climbed the tree— Racso with some difficulty, since he was still clutching the paper bag—and peered over the side into the nest. It looked clean and soft. They scrambled in, and each ate a light supper. As soon as they finished eating, they both lay down and closed their eyes.

But Timothy could not fall asleep. He remembered the chapter in the rats' history book, which described Jenner as tough, smart, and cynical. He had been the rat who had argued with Nicodemus, the leader; who had maintained that the rats had every right to steal food and electricity from the farmers. He had opposed the move to Thorn Valley as naive, arguing that the rats were entitled to a life of luxury without work, that the smartest animals always managed to take advantage of those who were less smart—in this case, Farmer Fitzgibbon. And when the rest of the community had sided with Nicodemus, Jenner and his six followers had left.

It was Timothy's mother who had first learned about the rats' death. She had overheard Mr. Fitzgibbon and his family discussing a newspaper article about some rats who had been electrocuted while they were trying to move a motor from the shelf of a hardware store. Scientists had come to town to investigate. Had the rats been trying to move the motor, they wondered, and if so, why? Could these rats be part of the intelligent group that had escaped from Nimh almost three years before? Were there others in the area?

So the accident had ended up endangering all the rats. Trying to collect specimens, the scientists had destroyed the nest under the rosebush. And two rats had died in that encounter. But since the move to Thorn Valley, the rats had been safe and happy. They had multiplied, grown their own crops, built their own shelter. Young rats went to school three seasons of the year. Timothy stirred in his bed. How would Racso fit into that community? Would he become like the other rats, cheerful and enthusiastic? Or would he be more like his father? These questions turned in Timothy's mind until finally sleep came, easing them away.

He awoke to bright sunlight and the sound of the river. He felt rested, and the sight of Racso sleeping on his back with paws curled up in the air made him laugh. The view from the nest was lovely: the forest floor carpeted with orange and yellow leaves, then the river, wide and shining in the sun. The water was high this season, higher than Timothy could ever recall. Had there been that much rain over the summer? Just as Timothy was trying to remember, Racso stirred, groaned, and sat up.

"What's for breakfast?" he asked.

"I've got beans and oats," Timothy said, "but I'd be willing to bet there'll be autumn olives down by the river. They're berries. Have you ever tasted them?"

"I think my mother brought some home from the market once, but I'm not sure."

"Come on," said Timothy, but then, remembering Racso's city upbringing, he added, "You always poke under the bushes first with a stick to make sure there aren't any snakes hiding there. Snakes can be very nasty."

"I'll remember that," Racso said. And Timothy noticed that he did use a long branch to stir up the leaves under each clump of berry bushes. When they finished eating, Racso picked extra berries and put them in his paper bag. "For lunch," he said. "They'll be perfect with the candy bars." And they set off down the path beside the river.

At first, they made good progress. The day was bright, but as the sun rose higher in the sky it became quite hot. Racso began to pant. "I'm thirsty," he complained. Another time he whined, "I'm too hot." Timothy realized that they would have to slow their pace. He had intended to reach the point where the river branched by evening, but that no longer seemed likely.

When the sun had passed a midpoint in the sky, they stopped for lunch. Racso ate three candy bars and all the berries he had picked, offering some to Timothy. He drank a great quantity of water from a small pool beside the river. Timothy ate only a few beans and a bit of fresh acorn.

They began to walk again. Racso walked more and more slowly. He was panting hard. Timothy tried walking a little ahead of him at a steady pace, but the rat fell farther and farther behind. Finally he stopped.

"I'm sorry," he said, "but I have to take a nap."

"Perhaps we could just sit down and rest for a minute," Timothy said.

"Sure," said the rat, but no sooner had they sat

down beside the path than Racso tumbled over onto the dry leaves and fell asleep.

He slept for two hours. When he awoke it was midafternoon. Timothy felt quite depressed. He didn't want to push the rat too hard; on the other hand, he certainly didn't want to miss the first day of school. Racso seemed to understand the problem, even though he was unaware of Timothy's deadline. "I'm afraid I'm used to sleeping during the day," he said. "In the city, we rats are most active at night, when the humans are asleep. I guess that's why being out in the sunlight makes me so tired."

"Country animals don't go out after dark if they can help it," Timothy said. "Owls hunt at night."

"I have only heard of owls," Racso said.

They walked on, keeping a steady pace, but it was not long before the sun disappeared behind the tall trees and the light began to fade. "We'll have to find a place to sleep," Timothy said. They searched among the trees and shrubs until they found shelter in a hollow log. It was damp, but clean. They ate moderately from their store of provisions and stretched out to go to sleep.

When Timothy awoke, it was still nighttime. Racso was standing at the opening of the log, looking out. He seemed glad to see Timothy awake. "I couldn't sleep," he said. "It's so beautiful out—there's a full moon! Come and look."

"What time is it?"

"I'm not sure."

Timothy went to the entrance of the log. The moon was high in the sky and cast a lovely light on the river and woods. The path was illuminated, almost as if it were day.

"I've never seen anything so beautiful!" Racso exclaimed. "In the city, on nights like this we all come out and play. You see rats everywhere . . . dancing, running, jumping. They call it moon fever."

"I've never been outside the house at night," said Timothy. Yet looking at the moon, he felt restless, as if he wanted to be out.

"I don't think I can go back to sleep," Racso said.

"I feel wide awake myself," Timothy said.

"I know that you're worried we didn't travel far enough today," Racso said. "I wouldn't mind walking a mile or two right now."

Timothy started to say no, for his mother had taught him that it is dangerous for a small animal to travel at night. On the other hand, they were way behind schedule, and it was clear that Racso would make better time at night, when it was cooler. And the moon was so bright that they should be able to spot any sign of danger, just as they would during the daytime. He struggled to decide. If they could walk two miles, they would probably reach the place where the river split; from there, it was only one day's travel to Thorn Valley.

"All right," he said. "But we'll have to be careful—really careful."

They gathered their supplies, and Timothy put on his knapsack. They climbed out of the log and across the leaves onto the path and began to walk. There was something magical about traveling through the semidarkness, with the moon shining overhead. Timothy felt as if he were entering a new world.

They hurried down the trail, passing from moonlight to darkness where overhanging trees shadowed the path. Racso sang happily in a low voice. It was the same song Timothy remembered him singing when they had first met: "Gonna find my baybee . . ." There were no signs of life anywhere.

After a bit, Racso stopped singing. Then Timothy noticed that it was extremely still. Besides the river and the padding of their own feet, he could hear nothing at all.

Racso was walking ahead of him on his left, in the shadow of the branches of an oak tree. Suddenly Timothy thought he saw the shadow move! Then it did move—it stretched, as if it had come alive! Timothy stopped, and as he stopped, the shadow moved to cover him and the spot where he stood. The moon was blotted out by huge, dark wings.

The shape fell toward Racso. A high-pitched scream filled the air. Racso could not move; he was paralyzed by fear. Timothy felt a scream come up in his own throat. He lunged and knocked Racso down. He fell over on his back on top of the rat. The bird hovered above them. His yellow eyes shone like moons. Timothy saw the great talons descending, and he felt pain. Before he fainted, he pushed one last breath of air from his chest, and he shouted his name: "TIMOTHY FRISBY!"

The owl hung in the air for another second. It shook the mouse from its foot with an angry cry. It rose in the dark, circled once, and flew away.

"He Was Your Son"

A note dropped from the sky near the Frisbys' home. Cynthia found it, a piece of paper folded neatly and tied with string to a small flat stone. The courier bird had been accurate; the packet had landed only a few feet from the entrance hole. Still, the sender had neatly printed an address on it, just in case:

Mrs. Jonathan Frisby
Cinder-block House
Fitzgibbon's Garden

Cynthia did not open the letter, but she was very excited. She carried it to her mother, who was down by the brook washing some bits of potato.

"MOTHER!" she shrieked. "We got a LET-TER!" She waved the little parcel in the air. "OPEN IT! OPEN IT RIGHT AWAY!"

Mrs. Frisby examined the packet carefully. She had little doubt where it had come from—the rats were the only animals she knew, besides her own family and Mr. Ages, who could read and write; but she suspected that they would not send her a message by air except in an emergency. Her paws shook a little as she untied the package and unfolded the letter. The message was written in a neat script in lavender ink that smelled like pokeberries.

Dear Mrs. Frisby,

Your son, Timothy, has not arrived for school as expected. If he will not be coming, please place a white stone one foot north of the entrance hole to your home.

Otherwise, we will search for him.

Sincerely,
Justin

"Who sent it? What does it say?" Cynthia asked. But when she saw her mother's downcast expression, she quieted. "What is it, Mother?"

"Timothy hasn't arrived at Thorn Valley," Mrs.

Frisby said. She tried to keep her voice calm but there were tears in her eyes.

"What day was he supposed to get there?" Cynthia asked. She counted on her whiskers: "He left five days ago, so he should have arrived yesterday. But Mother, they didn't know that he was coming on foot. And you know Timothy can dawdle."

"That's true," Mrs. Frisby said, though she did not really believe it.

"He'll get there," Cynthia said stubbornly.

Mrs. Frisby could see that her daughter was also fighting back tears. "Of course he will," she said, forcing a smile. "Let's not think about it until we get further news." And they agreed they would not.

But that evening a strange crow flew down from the sky and arrived at Mrs. Frisby's doorstep. He croaked twice, and when Mrs. Frisby appeared, he gestured toward his back.

"Who are you?" Mrs. Frisby asked.

The crow looked at her but did not answer.

She tried again, this time adding a note of false authority to her voice: "Who are you? Why are you here?"

Again, the crow refused to speak but merely gestured to his back.

Mrs. Frisby felt sure that the crow had something

to do with Timothy. She went back into the house, wrapped her shawl around her, and told the children that she had to run an errand. Then, resolving to think of Timothy alive and well, she climbed onto the strange crow's back.

The crow rose in the air and flew quickly over the farmer's field and above the forest. Mrs. Frisby did not open her eyes or look down. She had no idea in what direction he was flying or how long they had been in the air before he suddenly banked and descended, landing on the branch of a hollow tree.

Mrs. Frisby looked around. She was surrounded by pine woods. Directly in front of her was the trunk of the tree, which seemed to her as wide as the side of a house, and on it, a dark, plate-shaped opening: the owl's door.

She climbed down. She had been here once before, three years earlier, to ask the owl's advice when Timothy was sick and could not be moved from the cinder-block house before plowing time. The owl had listened to her then and had sent her to the rats for help. But she had felt terrified in his presence, for he was known among the animals as a fierce hunter and the wisest of all the creatures who lived in the meadows and woods.

She went to the edge of the opening and looked

inside. He was there, huge and terrible as he had
been before, his yellow eyes shining through the
dark. "Come in," he said. His voice sounded like
trees creaking in the wind.

Mrs. Frisby stepped into the hollow room. She
saw dimly the cavernous shapes of the dark chamber,
which reminded her of a vast tomb. Pieces of broken
wood formed a sort of walkway back toward the
owl's nest, where he was standing. Mrs. Frisby picked
her way along this jagged bridge until she stood
within a foot of the owl's great head.

"Mrs. Frisby." The owl's voice was very deep and
very sad. "You may wonder why I have sent for
you."

"Yes," she said. She was trembling.

"I have sent for you," the owl began, but then he
appeared to choke, and he began again: "I have sent
for you because I believe that I have killed your son."

So that was it. For a moment, Mrs. Frisby thought
that she was falling into the darkness, but later she
realized that her feet were on the wooden pathway
and that she was still standing in the owl's chamber.
She felt the tears flowing down her face.

"Two nights ago," the owl continued, "I went out
hunting in North Woods, where the river splits. I
was hungry and saw two rodents on the path in the

moonlight. I dove for the larger—a small rat—but the smaller one rushed to protect him. I picked him up, and he shouted his name." Here the owl paused. "Timothy Frisby," he said gently. "He was your son, was he not?"

Mrs. Frisby was overcome by grief. She nodded her head.

"I dropped him when I realized who he was," the owl said. "But I had grabbed him with my talons, and I am afraid that I pierced his heart."

There was silence in the chamber for a long time. Mrs. Frisby tried to hold her sobs deep in her throat. She could not speak.

"He died a hero, like his father," the owl said. "That may be some comfort to you."

Again, there was silence. A wind blew, and the dead limbs of the tree rattled like drumbeats. The old tree shook as if it would fly apart. Suddenly Mrs. Frisby realized she was no longer afraid. She felt as if she had lost all her strength: to fight, to work, even to fear.

The owl leaned down.

"You have other children," he said gently. "You must go home to them. You must prepare to make a long journey, away from this country. Men with great machines are working at the north end of Thorn

Valley. They are destroying the mountain there, and they plan to destroy the woods and farms as well."

Mrs. Frisby nodded, but it was hard for her to listen to the owl. What good was his warning now? Timothy was dead. That was all that mattered.

"I killed your son because I had to eat," the owl said. "There was a reason. With men, it often seems that there is no reason at all."

"Money," Mrs. Frisby said softly. She felt numb. "I have heard it said that men do what they do for pieces of paper called money."

The owl shook his great head, as if in puzzlement or sorrow. He turned his face toward the wall and did not speak again. Mrs. Frisby did not say good-bye but made her way slowly out to where the crow was waiting. She climbed onto his back.

"Fly to the North Woods, along the river," she told him. "Fly close to the ground, where there is a path. I am looking for someone there."

The crow's voice was low and rasping. "It is nearly dark."

"There will be moonlight," Mrs. Frisby said. She pulled her shawl around her shoulders and spoke as if she were in the habit of commanding crows. "Hurry! There is no time to lose."

[44]

The Struggle

The first thing that Timothy was aware of was the cold. Before he could speak, even before he could think a complete thought, he felt the cold. It seemed to come from inside his body, rather than from the air outside, and the various layers he could feel piled over him for warmth did not affect it. Sometimes his entire body would tremble, and after that he would feel a little better.

Later he heard a voice. He was sure that it was not his mother. The voice would say his name over and over in a sad, pleading tone: "Timothy, Timothy, Timothy." The voice would come into his mind and hold his attention for a very brief while, like the flickering flame of a candle. It was hard to listen. It was easier to sink back into the darkness.

But it seemed that the voice could rescue him from the cold. For that reason, it was important to try to listen to it and to hear what it was saying. Each time the voice came, Timothy struggled to hear it and to keep it in his mind: Someone is talking; someone is talking to me.

He had many dreams. He dreamed that his mother was with him and that she was speaking to him and saying his name. He dreamed that she put her paw upon his head and that she gave him soup. He dreamed about Thorn Valley. He dreamed that the school had opened and that the rats had failed to notice that he was missing. He could see Arthur standing at the front of the classroom, pointing to a diagram on the blackboard. His friends—Brendan, Sally, and Isabella—were in their seats. Racso was sitting in a desk in the front row. He could see his own desk: It was empty.

He dreamed that he had died. He dreamed that his mind left his body and rose in the air, and could fly. He could not fly as high or as fast as Jeremy; but by continued effort he could drift in whatever direction he wanted. He flew slowly above the trail in the forest. He saw birds and animals, but they could not see him. For a moment he thought that he would turn around and fly back toward his winter home in the cinder block; but he continued to drift, like a small loose ship on a calm sea.

The day he opened his eyes was the first day he felt the pain. He looked up and saw Racso's face looking down into his.

"You're alive," Racso said. His eyes filled with tears.

After that, the memories were mercifully jumbled. He remembered the rat pouring water into his mouth. Another time he woke up and tasted chocolate in his mouth and realized that Racso had been feeding him. Once he woke up and thought that he was alone, but when he turned his head slightly, he saw the rat sitting there beside him.

There was a horrible pain in his chest and shoulder. He did not have to move to feel it; he felt it all the time he was awake and sometimes, now, when he was sleeping. The pain throbbed, and sometimes it seemed to squeeze his entire body like a gigantic hand that was bent on crushing him. At those times he felt like screaming.

One time when he woke up his head felt clearer.

He saw Racso sitting beside him, and he spoke his name. The rat turned to him quickly and smiled. That night Timothy was aware of being fed, and he tried to swallow as much as he could, so that he would get stronger.

When he woke up the next morning, he remembered what had happened. They had been walking at night and had been attacked by an owl. The owl had grabbed him with its talons. The memory ended there. He wondered why he was still alive. "What day is this?" he asked. Racso explained that after the accident he had dragged Timothy off the trail onto a small shelf of rock in the side of a dry gully. The shelf was covered with leaves but bordered with rock on two sides, so that it broke the wind and hid them from view. He told Timothy they had been on the shelf for three full days.

"How much food is left?" Timothy asked.

"Don't worry about that," Racso said bravely. But Timothy thought that he looked a little scared.

That evening Racso brought Timothy small portions of beans and chocolate. "Tomorrow morning I want you to find a willow tree," Timothy told him. "They grow along the river. Willow bark relieves pain."

"I don't think I can recognize a willow tree," Racso said.

"I'll describe it, and you can take my knife to cut the bark off."

"Won't you be frightened if I leave you?"

"Yes," Timothy said, "but I want you to go. The sooner I feel better, the sooner we will be able to leave."

Later that night Timothy awoke to find himself covered with leaves. Racso was nestled close beside him. When he felt Timothy stir he whispered, "Don't move! There's a big bird flying back and forth over the path. I covered us both up with leaves so it couldn't see us. It's flown past again and again, as if it were searching for someone."

"Someone to eat," Timothy said grimly.

"It's calling somebody," Racso said. "And the funny part is, its voice doesn't sound like a bird. But I couldn't make out what it was saying."

Timothy wondered: Could it be the owl, returning for his prey? Owls had been known to trick all but the most cautious mice. He shivered in his bed of leaves. "We must stay hidden," he told Racso. And before long, he fell back to sleep.

The next morning Racso set off with the description of the willow bark and Timothy's small knife. In an hour he was back, bringing with him a variety of barks. Timothy recognized one as the willow bark he needed. He broke off a small bit and chewed it; almost immediately he fell back to sleep and slept for several hours. When he awoke he felt better.

"It's dangerous for us to camp here day after day," he told Racso. "We're certain to be noticed by other animals, and not all of them are friendly."

That night Racso brought Timothy a meal of ground oats. Timothy noticed that the rat did not eat anything at all. When he mentioned it, Racso said, "I ate earlier." But he looked tired.

Timothy decided that they should try to leave the next day. He chewed more of the willow bark and fell asleep. He slept deeply, without dreaming. Racso slept close beside him. When he awoke Racso was still asleep. Timothy rolled onto his stomach, gathered his hind legs under his body, then tried to ease a little weight onto his front legs. He was seized with pain. He clenched his teeth to keep from crying out. He tried again; again the pain was agonizing, and he slipped back down onto his stomach. He knew now that it would be some time before he would be able to walk.

He was filled with anger. How had he gotten into

this situation? It was all Racso's fault. He remembered the day he had left on his trip to Thorn Valley, how happy he had been. Life had seemed simple before he had met Racso. All he had wanted was to get to school on time.

He looked at Racso on the ground, breathing peacefully. He felt like hurting the rat, yet he knew he would have died without Racso's help. Angry tears welled up in Timothy's eyes.

Racso woke up. He looked at Timothy's position on the ground and guessed what had happened.

"You tried to walk."

Timothy nodded. He tried to control his tears, but he could not. Racso moved over beside him and touched his shoulder.

"Don't cry, Timothy," he said. "I got you into this mess, and I'm going to get you out of it. I've already decided what to do. I'm going to build a sling and pull you along the trail. I'll get you to Thorn Valley if it's the last thing I ever do."

Reunion

As Timothy's strength increased, Racso became less worried about him, and the rat grew cocky, as he had been when he and Timothy first met.

"Just leave it all to me," he told Timothy cheerfully. "Last year I snuck behind the baseboard at the movie theater and saw a show about how to live in the woods. It was called *The Last of the Mohicans*. There was an Indian in the movie who was kind of short for his age and looked a lot like me. And he made a sling to move his wounded friend."

"Animals who live in the wild have certain rules about how to act in the woods," Timothy said. "I've been thinking that it would be useful to review them with you."

"I probably know them all already," Racso said. "But you can tell me if it will make you feel better."

"The first one is *always cover up your trail*."

Racso shrugged as if the idea were nothing new. "Of course," he said. "I just happen to like to flip my tail around, that's all."

"I could tell where you'd walked," Timothy said. "That means an enemy could, too."

Racso pulled his hat down over his ears and didn't say anything.

"The second rule is this," Timothy said. *"If you hear something coming, even from far away, take cover."*

"I hid us from that bird the other night, didn't I?" Racso chuckled. "And that bird was looking for someone—even in the dark I could tell that. It flew back and forth over the path, again and again!"

Timothy stared, troubled and uncertain. What if that bird had *not* been the owl, as he had suspected? He thought of Jeremy—but no, Jeremy was at his mother's. And anyway, how could he have known that Timothy was in trouble? The whole thing was probably just Racso's imagination. And it was up to him to bring Racso down to earth. He shook his head in disgust.

"Here's another rule," he said gruffly. *"Never light a fire in the woods."*

Now Racso was ready to argue.

"The Indians did."

"We're not Indians," Timothy said. "Anyway, they were *careful*. They knew how to make a fire without setting the woods on fire."

"So do I," Racso said defensively. "I toasted marshmallows the night before I met you. I melted chocolate squares right in the middle of the marshmallow. The Girl Scouts do that, you know. It's a famous dessert."

"RACSO!" Timothy felt totally exasperated. "I put that fire out myself the next morning! You could have burned the whole forest down and killed us both!"

Racso looked surprised and then concerned.

"You'd better rest now," he suggested. "You're getting upset over nothing, Timothy." He smiled beneficently. "And if there's one thing we don't need right now, it's a worried little field mouse!"

Racso spent all morning working on the sling. He used Timothy's knife to cut and trim two four-inch sticks. He stretched Timothy's jacket between the two sticks, buttoned it, and ran the sticks through the coat sleeves. He fastened the sleeves to the body of the jacket with string, and wove the string back and forth under the jacket like a hammock. After that he used another string to fashion a simple harness for himself.

"Wrap the ends of this around your paws a couple of times, so that it can't slip out," he told Timothy, handing him the traces of the harness. "When you're ready I'll get up on all fours and run up the bank as quickly as I can. It may hurt, but at least it should be over with fast."

Timothy did as he was told. He felt pain, but he held on, realizing that the worst would soon be over. Still, when they reached the trail he felt faint and sick to his stomach. He lay still for a long time.

Racso fed him a portion of oats. Timothy could see that the corn-husk wrapper in which the oats had been packed was now empty. He chewed some willow bark and drank a bit of water. He lay back on the sling and tried to rest. Racso fastened the knapsack to the sticks just under Timothy's hind feet.

"We're ready to go," he said.

"Where's the paper bag?" Timothy asked.

"It's empty," Racso said, looking away.

He fitted the two sticks onto loops in the string

and began to pull. The sticks slid over the ground easily. Timothy lay back and tried to relax. Although his chest and shoulder throbbed, he could lie quietly in the sling as it moved, and the ride over the path was quite smooth.

Racso pulled Timothy along the trail for almost an hour. Although the sun was behind a cloud, the day was warm, and Racso's fur was slick with sweat. "I have to rest awhile," he told Timothy. He sat down and drank some water. He looked hesitantly at Timothy. "Did you once mention that your family ate acorns?" He said the last word with a grimace, as if it offended him.

Timothy spotted an oak tree and pointed to it. "Look under there," he said. "There will be hundreds of acorns on the ground. Bring me a couple, and I'll show you how to eat them."

Racso searched under the tree and returned with two large acorns. One of them was already cracked. Timothy pulled it apart and took out the juicy inner kernel. He ate a little bit himself and then handed the rest to Racso. Racso took a huge bite and chewed briefly, but instead of swallowing the acorn, he spit it out on the ground. "It's *bitter*," he complained. Then, sadly, he took another bite, gulping hurriedly. He ate bite after bite. "I like berries," he said when he had finished the entire nut, "but I *don't* like acorns."

They traveled for another hour. The ground was still quite smooth, and the fallen leaves cushioned the bumps. Timothy felt tired, but the sound of the river flowing nearby was soothing. Still, he worried about Racso. He suspected that the rat had not had enough to eat for several days. And it was clear that the store of provisions they had brought with them was almost exhausted.

Suddenly Racso gave a whoop. He turned around to Timothy with a smile. "We've reached the spot where the river splits," he said. "I can see a large stream flowing off to the left." The sling was too low to the ground for Timothy to see, but he was pleased. The trail turned north, and they followed it.

It began to get dark. They decided to sleep in the midst of a large honeysuckle thicket. Racso divided the curtain of vines enough to slip the sling through it into an open, central room. It was quite dark, but airy and dry, with a faint sweet odor of rotted honeysuckle blooms.

"I'm hungry," Racso said sadly.

"Is there any food left in the knapsack?"

"It's for you."

Timothy opened the knapsack and looked inside.

He found a packet with two beans in it and a small square of chocolate. Timothy ate one of the beans, and offered the candy to Racso.

"You eat it," Racso said.

"I like the beans just as much."

Racso hesitated.

"Here," Timothy said, handing him the chocolate, and the rat gobbled it down gratefully.

In the morning, they shared the last bean in the knapsack and headed north. The leaves swirled around Timothy, and occasionally Racso batted them higher into the air with his tail. Suddenly Racso stopped stock-still. "I thought I heard something," he whispered. Timothy listened, too. Sure enough, from someplace far ahead on the path there came a slight rustling noise. Was it the wind? Timothy could not be sure.

"Let's hide," Racso said.

He pulled the sling to a sheltered spot behind the trunk of a large pine tree and crouched down. The rustling continued and grew louder. Racso peeped out from behind the tree. "I don't see anything," he told Timothy.

"Shhhh!" Timothy said. The rustling grew louder still.

The rat peeked out again. Timothy saw his body grow stiff with excitement. "What is it, Racso?" he whispered. "What do you see?"

"Rats," Racso whispered. His voice was trembling. "Four large rats."

Timothy's eyes grew wide. "What do they look like? Lift me up, so I can see."

Racso lifted the sling so that it leaned against the tree trunk like a short ladder. Timothy craned his neck. Still, he could not see the rats. "More, more!" he whispered, and Racso leaned the sling a little farther to one side.

The rats were standing in a circle on the path, about forty feet to the north of the pine tree. They were talking, but Timothy could not see their faces. Then suddenly the leader moved so that he was facing the tree.

"Justin," Timothy whispered to himself; and then he yelled, "JUSTIN!"

Racso panicked. "TIMOTHY! Be quiet! What are you doing?"

"JUSTIN!" Timothy yelled again, joyfully.

The rat looked toward the tree. Then he began to run.

"He's coming right this way!" Racso groaned.

"JUSTIN!" Timothy shouted.

"Take cover!" Racso yelled. "He's going to kill us both!"

Just at that moment the rat burst from behind the tree. Racso threw himself facedown on the ground, covered his head with his paws, and curled up into a ball.

"Justin!" shouted Timothy.

"Timothy!" the large rat said. He embraced the mouse and signaled the other rats to come. "Thank goodness!" he said. "We've found you at last!"

Welcome to Thorn Valley

Racso was unusually quiet during the introductions. He noticed that Justin spoke less than the other rats but that when he did speak, the others listened. Racso felt strongly that he wanted to make a good impression on Justin, and he was mad at Timothy for letting him make a fool of himself.

Brutus, the largest and strongest of the four rats, was friendly but bumbling. He started to pick Timothy up to embrace him but was stopped by Justin, who felt the embrace might do Timothy more harm than good. Brendan, the youngest, clapped Timothy on the head affectionately and told him about the first day of class. "When you didn't show up, we knew something was wrong," he said. "Then we heard about Jeremy's mother, and we realized you'd be coming on foot. We decided to wait three more days before we started looking. We even sent a message to your mother at Fitzgibbon's."

"She'll be worried," Timothy said.

"We'll let her know you've been found," Justin said.

"Poor Timothy!" Isabella, the only female in the group, was indignant. "I *hate* owls! Don't you, Justin?"

Justin didn't answer her. "We should prepare to return to Thorn Valley," he said. "If we leave here now, we can arrive there by nightfall."

They agreed that Brutus and Brendan would take turns pulling the sling, and that they would trade off with Justin and Isabella. Racso would wear Timothy's knapsack to lighten the load on the stretcher. They set off down the path at a steady clip.

After several hours, Racso realized that they had forgotten to stop for lunch. His stomach was growling, and he was beginning to feel tired. At the same time he felt embarrassed. No one else seemed to feel tired or hungry. He wondered if Timothy was hungry. He reminded himself that the mouse had only eaten half a bean for breakfast. But when he went alongside the stretcher he discovered that Timothy was asleep.

He slipped back to walk beside Isabella. At first, she continued to walk straight ahead, with her eyes forward. Then after a while she looked a little to the side. And she looked as if she wanted to laugh.

"Is something funny?" Racso asked.

Isabella choked back a giggle. "Oh, no," she said airily. "Nothing at all."

"What is it?" Racso insisted.

"If you must know," Isabella said haughtily, "it's your hat! Where in the world did it come from?"

"Out of a trash can," Racso explained. He felt hurt. He had always thought the hat made him look somewhat distinctive, and it definitely made him look taller. "My dad said it used to belong to a doll. It fits me perfectly, don't you think?"

Instead of answering, Isabella began to giggle out loud.

"What's so funny?" said Racso. He was beginning to feel angry. "Don't you have any HATS at Thorn Valley?"

Isabella was trying to stop laughing but she couldn't.

Then, to make matters worse, Justin turned from the head of the procession and signaled for them to be quiet. Racso was furious. He felt that Isabella had caused him to be humiliated; but to his surprise, Isabella was just as angry as he was. "You got me in trouble with *Justin*," she hissed.

Racso slunk to the end of the line. These Thorn Valley rats think they know it all, he thought bitterly. I've traveled all this way to find them, and they act as if they don't even care. And Isabella reminds me of my sister. Yet he had to admit that she was quite an attractive rat.

Justin signaled for them to stop. He disappeared into the woods ahead, then returned and gathered the rats into a circle around him.

"We have only about one mile to go before we reach Thorn Valley," he said quietly. "But that mile is the most difficult part of our trip. We must cross over the mountain and descend into the valley, and there are only about three hours of daylight left." He paused. "We must decide now whether we want to finish the journey this afternoon, or whether we should camp for the night and arrive tomorrow morning."

"I can go faster," Brutus said. "Timothy is very light."

"I'm ready to go on," Brendan said. "I'm not as strong as Brutus, but I'll pull the sling for as long as I can."

"I'll do whatever *you* want to do, Justin," Isabella said.

All eyes turned toward Racso. "Uhh," Racso said. He could hardly keep from panting even now that the group had stopped. He wished desperately that Timothy would wake up. Then, before he could speak, his stomach growled. Isabella started to giggle, but Justin silenced her with a glance.

"Pulling the sling by yourself must have been tiring," he said kindly. "Let's stop and eat, and rest for a while. Then you can decide whether you want us to go on with the journey tonight."

Racso decided that he liked Justin very much. He sat down on the ground next to him and deliberately did not look toward Isabella. Brutus opened the knapsack and passed around a packet of raw spinach and some bits of carrot. Racso was not overly fond of spinach, but he took a large portion. He noticed that the other rats ate sparingly and without speaking. They passed water around in a pouch made of animal skin, and each drank in turn. Racso drank, too.

At the end of the meal Justin turned to him. "How do you feel now?"

Racso did not hesitate. "Much better," he said. "I'm ready to go on."

Justin thought for a moment before he spoke. "The sooner we get medical care for Timothy, the better off he'll be," he said. "On the other hand, it's going to be hard for you to finish this journey today. You haven't had the physical training that we have, and the mountain trail is steep." He paused.

"This is my suggestion," he said. "Brendan, you walk with Racso. If he gets too tired, the two of you should camp overnight and finish the trip tomorrow."

Racso felt all the more determined to get to Thorn Valley with the rest. He tried to assume the more alert bearing he had observed in the other rats and to move his feet lightly, so that they did not make a crunching sound in the leaves. And he refrained from flipping his tail.

Abruptly the trail changed and became more rocky. Often, to remain on the path it was necessary for the rats to scramble over sharp stones. Justin, still in the lead, took out a rope and tied it around his chest. He passed it back and, in turn, each rat let out a length and then looped the rope around himself and passed it on.

Brendan helped Racso fasten the rope around him.

"We do this in case one of us should slip," he explained. "If you feel someone falling, grab on to the rock nearest you and hold on tight."

They came to the base of a stone formation. Brendan told Racso that it was the peak of the mountain. The view from the trail was beautiful: Racso could see miles of woodland and the river, which wound through the trees like a green ribbon. They took off the safety ropes, and Brendan stood beside him as they looked out over the forest.

"Look how the river's flooded to the north there," Brendan pointed out. "Justin says we have to find out why. We might even send out an exploring party."

"I could be one of the leaders!" Racso said cheerfully. "I know a lot about the woods, and about scouting. I learned it from a movie about the Indians."

Brendan looked as if he were about to say something, but instead of words it came out as a slight choking sound, almost like a giggle. Racso looked hard at Brendan, but Brendan just nodded politely.

The two rats hurried to catch up. They walked along a ledge about six inches wide. Racso was frightened, but he decided to pretend that he was running along a sewer pipe at home. Suddenly the trail widened and began to go down.

"Not long now," Brendan said.

Racso could hardly keep his eyes on the trail. He saw a valley spread out below him. The setting sun, reflecting off the stone wall of the mountain, cast a golden light over the fields and trees. Racso looked for houses, buildings, lights; but they were nowhere. He looked for busy hordes of rats, but he did not see them. He was puzzled.

Twilight fell. It was too dark to search for the civilization at Thorn Valley. Racso felt extremely tired. He put one foot in front of the other—one, two, one, two—and kept his eyes on Brendan's back. They continued downward. Racso knew that his journey was almost over. He was too exhausted to be happy or even relieved. He wanted to go to bed. He remembered vaguely all the times his father had tried to make him go to bed, and how he had argued. The trail continued downward. The other rats were silent. Racso felt as if he were walking in a dream.

Justin whistled, a long piercing sound resembling a bird's cry. Another whistle floated back through the dark. They turned and walked over something that felt like gravel chips. There was no moon. Racso could not see anything. Then he felt Brendan touch his shoulder: "This way." They went through a gully and entered what looked like an ordinary rat hole. It was dark, and there was the smell of mud. The passage twisted and turned.

Suddenly Racso saw light ahead of them. He thought he heard voices and laughter. He hurried along behind Brendan. The passageway ended in a large, bright room. Racso saw rats—a hundred rats. Someone handed him a wooden cup filled with broth, and he drank deeply. It warmed his throat and belly.

Then he noticed that the crowd of rats had formed a loose circle, with him and Brendan and Timothy inside it. Beside Justin was an older rat wearing a black eye patch, and next to him a small, lively-looking female with a long black tail. They were looking at him. He felt shy, but he flipped his tail boldly in the air and adjusted his hat over his ears. He wanted to look his best.

Brendan came and stood at his shoulder. "The rat with the eye patch is Nicodemus," he whispered. "He's the founder of the community. He's nice, but he's strict."

"What about the female?"

"She's Hermione. We elected her to be Presiding Rat this year—to call the meetings and make sure everyone gets a chance to speak. You'll get to know her, because she's the schoolteacher. And Justin is the head of Rat Security."

At that moment, the rat called Nicodemus stepped forward. The circle grew silent as he approached Racso. His one eye regarded Racso sternly, but there was warmth in his voice:

"We welcome you to the community of Thorn Valley, Racso," he said. "We hope your visit with us will be a pleasant one. We do not often have visitors from the outside world, and we are always eager to learn what is happening there. For our life at Thorn Valley has made us a bit isolated, you see."

He hesitated, and his voice became softer, less formal.

"Thank you for taking care of Timothy when he was hurt," he said. "I shall write to my dear friend Mrs. Frisby tonight to let her know that he is here, and I shall mention your part in caring for him and bringing him here."

"Thank you," said Racso.

Nicodemus turned to Timothy, who looked cheerful and bright-eyed. He placed one paw on Timothy's head. "As for you," he said smiling, "I hear that you've made yourself a hero. And knowing your father as I did, and also Mrs. Frisby, I'm not surprised. Welcome back, Timothy. We hope you'll have a good year at school."

There was a murmur among the rats as the formal

greetings ended. Nicodemus, Timothy, and Brendan talked together in low tones. Racso did not even notice that he was alone. He was thinking: thinking about the fact that Nicodemus had said Timothy was a hero. But what about him, Racso? Hadn't he dragged Timothy on the sling until he nearly passed out? Hadn't he shared his chocolate with Timothy? And why had Nicodemus referred to his stay at Thorn Valley as a "visit"? Didn't he know that Racso was here to stay?

But he thought about these things only for a moment, because Isabella came and said, "Justin says to show you to your bed. You'll be sharing a room with Timothy." Racso followed gratefully as she led him out the door and down the long clay hallway. He was too tired to care that she didn't glance back to make sure he was behind her, or say good night. Tomorrow he would explore, and meet more rats, and learn more about Isabella . . . but tonight, tonight was for sleeping.

Nicodemus

Racso slept late. When he rolled over on his bed of soft rushes he saw that Timothy's bed was already empty. He stretched and looked around. Light filtered through a high window in the small room, so that by daylight it was quite cheerful. Besides the two beds, the room contained a wooden shelf and a series of pegs, from two of which hung Racso's hat and Timothy's knapsack. The clay floor was clean and dry, and the walls had been painted with lime to make them brighter. The door was wooden, with an arched top. It was open.

Where was Timothy? Racso half remembered Justin saying that Timothy would see the doctor this morning. Could he be there already? But as Racso considered going to look for him, Brendan appeared in the doorway.

"Good morning, Racso. Did you sleep well?"

Racso nodded.

"I'll bet you're hungry. I'm going to take you to the cafeteria for breakfast. After that you'll get the whole tour."

"Just let me get my hat and slick my fur down. . . ." Racso brushed his ears and whiskers with his front paws and adjusted his beret. He followed Brendan down a long hallway, passing many doors that looked just like the door to his own room.

"The bedrooms were built along a high bank, so that they could be lighted by the sun or moon," Brendan explained. "Some of the storerooms on the inside tier have no windows. We light those with beeswax candles."

Racso was disappointed. "I thought you'd have electric lights."

"We used to, when the colony lived under the rosebush at the Fitzgibbons'," Brendan said. "I was too little to remember, but I've heard the others talk about it. But we were stealing electricity from the farmers, and the leaders didn't think it was right to do that."

Racso had heard about this decision from Jenner, but he'd imagined that the rats would have changed their minds by now. He loved the magical feeling of turning on a light switch in a darkened room, as he loved the other products of electricity: stereos, TVs, telephones. In the city he had envied the electronic gadgets carried by humans: radios that sat on ears like little black earmuffs; huge silver radios carried by kids on their bikes, blaring wonderful music. Then there were the tape decks, the calculators with their shimmering green digits, movie projectors that could create another world on a screen or a white sheet. He had hoped the rats at Thorn Valley would have cars and motorcycles. He had thought there would be a playroom with video games and pinball machines. And surely they would have a computer in the classroom! He looked around nervously. If the technological revolution had come to Thorn Valley, he could see no sign of it so far.

He followed Brendan into the cafeteria, a wide room with a long series of windows. There were stacks of wooden bowls along one wall, with names on them; along another wall were baskets filled with nuts, seeds, carrots, onions, turnips, and dried fruits. In an adjacent room stood a big clay oven and a fireplace.

"We use those mostly in colder weather," Brendan explained. "The soup we made last night was special, for Timothy's homecoming."

Timothy! You would think he was a movie star the way they talked about him! Racso felt jealous. He selected food for his breakfast and ate greedily, although he was not fond of vegetables and fruit: Health food, he would have called it at home.

"Where are the others?" he asked Brendan, between mouthfuls.

Brendan looked surprised. "We get up with the sun," he said. "Most of the colony is hard at work by now: gardening, harvesting, gathering wood, weaving baskets, digging up the ground for a new water main. The babies are in the nursery—that's just down the hall and to the left—and of course, the young rats are in school. I'm to take you to see Nicodemus. Then I'll go back to school myself."

School! At last Racso was to get his chance to learn to read and write! He wanted to tell Brendan not to take him to see Nicodemus, just take him right to the classroom.

They went back into the hallway. "If you don't mind, I'll go past my room and pick up my books," Brendan said.

Racso nodded. But when Brendan emerged from his room, Racso's eyes opened wide. In a book bag woven of dried vines, Brendan had not just one book, but three. He had two quill pens and paper made from birch bark. Racso eyed them greedily.

"Would you give me a pen, since you have more than one?" he asked politely.

"No," Brendan answered, just as politely. "You must make your own. Until you do, you'll write on the floor with a sharp stick. All the beginners learn that way."

Racso felt hurt and angry. He had thought rats at Thorn Valley would be willing to share! Suddenly he noticed that one of the quill pens had slipped down near the bottom on the book bag, so that it was hanging partway out. He reached quickly and snatched it.

"Hey, Racso!" Brendan yelled. "Give that back."

"Give what back?" Racso asked. He tried to look innocent, and held the pen behind him with his back leg.

"Give me my pen!"

"You really don't need *two* pens," Racso said persuasively. "You can't write with both paws at once, can you?"

Before Brendan could answer, around the corner came Nicodemus.

Racso wouldn't have thought a rat like Brendan would be a tattletale, but he was wrong. Brendan told the whole story to Nicodemus. Racso felt like disappearing. He decided it would be better not to argue when Nicodemus said, "Give him his pen immediately, Racso. And you, Brendan, you go on to school."

Racso walked with Nicodemus to his office.

"Please sit down. I'll join you in a moment," the head rat said solemnly.

Racso was scared. He went into the room and sat in a straight chair beside a wooden desk. The office was small and tidy, with a red rug on the floor and sketches hanging from the walls. Besides the desk and extra chair, there was a bookcase packed with books and notebooks, and on the bottom shelf, a shiny metal box with knobs on it—a radio! At least one rat here was up-to-date. Racso loved music. He took pride in the number of lyrics he could sing from the golden oldies and top hit list.

Nicodemus came in and sat behind the desk. He

did not look directly at Racso. "Tell me about yourself," he said quietly.

Racso was not sure what to tell, or where to begin.
If Nicodemus was still angry with Jenner, might he
prefer that Jenner's son stay away from Thorn Valley? What if he made Racso leave? The thought of
having to travel all the way home was terrible. He
decided to lie.

"I was born in the city," he said in a small voice.
"My family is very poor and lives in the basement
wall of an abandoned house. My father works all
night hauling garbage from the central market to an
orphanage of little rats whose parents died from rat
poisoning. But he wants me to have an education,
so he sent me here."

Racso paused and considered his story. He liked
the part about the orphaned rats—that sounded goody-
goody, which Nicodemus would probably go for—
but the ending was weak. How would his father
have known about Thorn Valley? He could see that
Nicodemus looked puzzled. Racso plunged ahead.

"A strange rat came to the orphanage and told my
father about Thorn Valley—that there was a school
here, and plenty of food. And this year my parents
decided I was old enough to come."

A frown creased Nicodemus's forehead, and he

closed his eyes partway as if he were scrutinizing a stone that might or might not be of some value. "But how did you know how to get here?"

Racso had not thought of that. He tried to be casual. "I followed the highway to Smithville, and then I found out where the Fitzgibbons live, and I met a big crow over there."

Racso noticed that Nicodemus was staring at him, and the stare was angry. "I gave the crow a shiny cigarette paper, and he told me where to go," he said lamely. "And then I met Timothy. . . ."

Nicodemus leaned over his desk and grabbed Racso by the scruff of his neck. He lifted him easily, as if Racso were just a sack of grain. "I don't have any use for liars," he said. "I'm going to set you outside, and you can go back where you came from."

"No," Racso said. "I don't want to." He scrambled to escape, but his paws treaded air. "Put me down. Please."

"Will you tell the truth this time?"

"Yes." Racso's neck was starting to hurt. "Please."

Nicodemus lowered him gently to the ground and returned to his chair as if nothing had happened. Racso got up. He was embarrassed, and his neck really hurt. Nicodemus was stronger than he looked. Racso sat down in his chair and looked at the floor.

"Well?"

"Jenner is my father," Racso blurted. "I know you don't like each other anymore, but please let me stay here anyway. . . . I really want to learn to read and write." He expected Nicodemus to get mad at him, but when he glanced at the older rat, he was surprised. Nicodemus's mouth was open and his face was blank with astonishment.

"Jenner! Do you mean that he's *alive*?"

Racso nodded. "He was the only one who survived the accident."

"Alive!" Nicodemus shook his head as if the news were difficult to accept. "Where is he now?"

"At home, in the city."

"If only we had known, we could have helped him. The papers said there were seven dead. . . ."

"He managed to creep away. He was badly burned, but he lay in a deserted basement while his wounds healed," Racso said. "There wasn't anything to eat. By the time he was strong enough to crawl out the window, he was practically starving."

"My poor friend. . . ." Nicodemus put his face between his paws. He stayed that way for several moments. When he took his paws down Racso was surprised to see that the fur under his good eye was wet.

"What happened then?" Nicodemus asked.

"He crawled along the ditch beside the highway until he was strong enough to walk, and then he walked until he came to the city. When he found my mother, he was covered with scars."

"If only we had known . . ." Nicodemus shook his head again. "We could have gone after him and brought him back. We could have kept him in the infirmary until he was well."

Racso didn't know what to say. Nicodemus had said to be honest, but he wasn't sure that Nicodemus would want to hear the truth. Finally he said, "It's better that you didn't."

"Why?"

Racso paused. "I was born after the accident, so I don't know what he was like before the accident. But my mother says he's changed. He's bitter and scared at the same time. He won't go out of the nest, because he doesn't want the others to see his scars, and whenever we go out, he gets scared."

"Scared of what?"

It was hard for Racso to answer that. "I'm not sure. He's scared that something will hurt us—a car, a person, another animal. He even worries that a telephone pole will fall on us, or a building will topple while we're inside looking for food."

"Paranoia," Nicodemus muttered. He shook his head sadly.

"He didn't want me to learn to read," Racso said. "He felt that the more I learned, the more dangerous my life would become, because I would want to learn even more, and see more. . . . He wanted me to stay in the rat hole with him, and eat garbage and sleep. But I couldn't do that."

"So you ran away?"

Racso nodded. He felt ashamed of what he said next, but he couldn't help himself. "I don't want the others to know."

"Know what?"

"About Jenner. That he's my father."

Nicodemus looked surprised. "Why not?"

"Because he left. . . . Because he was a trouble-maker. . . ."

Nicodemus regarded Racso gravely. "Your father had strong convictions and he followed them. That takes courage."

"He doesn't have any friends now," Racso said. "He doesn't care about anyone. Only me, and my mother and sister."

"He must love you a great deal," Nicodemus said. "I shall try to send him a message, so that he'll know you arrived here safely. And since you've requested it, I won't tell the others about Jenner."

"Timothy already knows."

"Yes, Timothy . . ." Nicodemus's voice became crisp, businesslike. "I wrote to Mrs. Frisby this morning. Our doctor, Elvira, thinks that he will make a quick recovery. We appreciate your taking such good care of him."

"Thank you."

"As for you . . ." Nicodemus paused. "We haven't talked about whether you should stay."

Racso had never really considered the possibility that he would not stay at Thorn Valley. For a moment he was at a loss for words. Finally he said weakly, "I want to stay."

"Why?" Nicodemus asked.

Racso hesitated. He wanted to speak well, but he was scared. After a while he said, "I want to be a scientist. I want to be a hero, like you."

Nicodemus looked genuinely startled. He laughed briefly. His good eye was open wide, and he regarded Racso with quiet amusement. "I am *not* a hero," he said. "And Thorn Valley is not in the business of raising heroes. Heroes are creatures of adversity—war, fire, accident, or disaster. Our dreams for Thorn Valley don't include the tragic circumstances that produce heroes. What we want is a community where rats cooperate to provide food and shelter, where work and pleasure are part of everyone's life."

"But you'll need heroes," Racso argued. "You'll need leaders."

"Leaders, yes," Nicodemus nodded. "But leaders are no more heroic than the rat who carries more grain than she really has to, or the student who does not lose his temper when another rat takes what is rightfully his."

There was silence in the office. Abruptly Nicodemus stood up. "I have to go see if Arthur's back," he said. "He's our chief engineer. He went with a few others to the Trout River to check on the flooding there, and he's due to return this morning." He turned as he was leaving. "I won't be long. Perhaps you'd like to sit here and think until I come back."

So Racso was alone. For a moment he sat quietly in his chair. Then he swung his feet back and forth. He tried to read the letters in the titles of Nicodemus's books. He started to get down off the chair. Then he remembered that he was supposed to be thinking. He tried to think, but his mind was completely blank. The more he tried to think, the more he couldn't think. Suddenly he remembered the way he had acted with Brendan. To be caught stealing in front of Nicodemus!

Then there had been the lie about his father. Sure, it made sense to think that Nicodemus might still be angry with Jenner. But Nicodemus had seemed to know that he was lying almost from the start. And then it turned out that Nicodemus still liked Jenner, after all, and was happy that he was alive. So the lie had made Racso look bad, too.

After a few moments, Nicodemus came back into the office.

"By the way," Racso said, trying to sound casual, "I hope you didn't notice the way I acted with Brendan this morning. I wasn't feeling well, and I lost my head."

Nicodemus looked surprised. "I see."

"And as far as what I said about my father working for the orphanage, that was wrong. I should have told you the truth to start with. But it won't happen again."

"I expect it will happen again," Nicodemus said, in a voice as casual as Racso's. "Since you are used to having your own way, it will be hard for you to change. I think you'll find it quite challenging, perhaps as challenging as more romantic activities, like mountain climbing or saving damsels in distress."

"I would like to do those, too," Racso said seriously.

Nicodemus laughed out loud. "And perhaps, in time, you will," he said.

Suddenly there was a pounding on the office door. Before Nicodemus could get up to open it, it was flung open, and a slight, wiry rat stood in the doorway.

"Nolan!"

"We're back from the river. And the news is bad—very bad. Arthur sent me to tell you."

"What is it?"

"We measured the rate at which the river's rising. If it continues like this, Thorn Valley will be underwater by Christmas!"

The Surveillance Parties

In the classroom all eyes were on Racso.

"Q . . . R . . . S, T . . . U . . . V," he recited, "W . . . X . . . Y . . . Z."

"That's wonderful! You've learned a lot in just three weeks, Racso." Hermione smiled.

Today Racso was paired with Amos, who was also learning to write and recite the alphabet. Timothy and Sally were putting the finishing touches on a map of the territory around the nest. After three weeks, Timothy still wore a soft bandage around his side, but the wound it covered had become a long, pink scar.

"We're finished!" Sally waved the large square of birch-bark paper in the air. "Come and look at what we've done!"

The other rats gathered around. Racso stood near the front of the group, because he was so short. The map was painted in vivid colors: blue for the water, greens for the meadows and gardens, browns and grays for the woods and mountains.

"I can see Emerald Pond!"

"There's the playground!"

"And here are the entrances to the nest—the front door, the back door, and the emergency door."

Sally nodded. She pointed to a wavy blue line. "Here's where the creek flows out of the Trout River and winds around until it gets to the dam at the pond . . . and here's the swimming hole . . . and here's the spot where we catch crayfish—you can tell because there's a bend toward the south right there."

Racso winced when Sally said the word "river." How could she seem so cheerful when they were all in danger? The phrase "underwater by Christmas" echoed in his mind. Yet the discussions in the classroom had been calm and rational, except for Racso.

"But I can't swim!" he would shout. "What am I going to do? Who will save me?"

Hermione tried to be reassuring. "We've faced other problems, Racso, and we've always found solutions. Just last fall we invented a trap to catch a red-tailed hawk who had built a nest on the cliff north of here. We blindfolded her and carried her to the other side of the mountain, where we let her go. And no one got hurt."

"But what about a life preserver?" Racso yelled.

The other students laughed out loud.

"Maybe Timothy will save you again," Brendan suggested archly. He hadn't forgotten the time when Racso had tried to take his pen.

Racso glared. "Just leave Timothy out of this!" he snapped.

Hermione was sympathetic. She saw Racso working hard and trying to be friendly with the other rats. But the stories about his girlfriends back in the city didn't impress the others. And when he sang the hit song "Everybody Jump in My Little Chevrolet," all the rats clapped politely, but no one asked him to sing it again.

He became so desperate to make an impression that he lied. He told the others that his family was rich and lived in the basement of a mansion with a swimming pool. Everyone just listened, except Timothy, who rolled his eyes. That made Racso even angrier. Timothy was Mr. Perfect—he never did anything wrong. Sometimes Racso felt like doing something mean to him, just for the fun of it. But he didn't dare. Timothy was his only friend.

Timothy enjoyed showing Racso the valley. The rats' nest was a complicated maze that took a full day to explore: the sleeping wing, the cafeteria, the storerooms, the nursery, the meeting room, the school. On the floor below these were an infirmary and several offices: one for Elvira the doctor, one for Nicodemus, one for Hermione, one for Arthur, one for Justin. There were three empty rooms with soft feather pillows and slate blackboards—"thinking rooms." These could be reserved by anyone who had a problem and needed a quiet place to figure out a solution. Some interesting inventions had been conceived there: the granite solar collectors, which heated the nest during the coldest part of the winter, and the water wheel, which produced energy and also ground acorns into flour and squeezed oil from the harvest of peanuts and soybeans.

But best of all was the playground.

"Is it really just for *us*?" Racso asked Timothy when he first saw it. "The ones I've seen have always been for human kids!"

Timothy nodded. "Arthur helped us build it last spring. The whole class worked on it together."

"I want to go on the slide!" Racso yelled. "I want to swing on the grapevine!"

"Go ahead," Timothy said. "There's only one rule—that we take turns. Everyone gets to go once before anyone goes twice."

That was hard for Racso. As he climbed the bamboo ladder to the polished wooden slide, he felt a rising excitement. Christopher had rubbed the chute with peanut oil to make it really fast. When he pushed off from the ladder, Racso felt as if he were flying! He slid down on all fours, then sitting upright, then belly up, with his tail waving. That was when Hermione reminded him of the rule.

"But I don't like to take turns!" he protested. "And anyway, the others had lots of turns before I ever got here. I need a chance to catch up!"

But Hermione insisted. So Racso waited in line impatiently, his hat jammed over his ears and his tail twitching. When his turn came, he scrambled up the ladder like a wild thing, then shrieked for joy during the fast ride down.

"There's a meeting tonight!" Hermione made the announcement just as school was about to be dismissed. "We'll be talking about the flooding, and trying to figure out what to do."

"Do the children go?" Racso asked.

"Of course. We couldn't possibly make a decision as a group without having the children there."

"Will we vote about what to do?"

Hermione hesitated. "Only if there is widespread disagreement. Usually, after a long discussion, we agree among ourselves on what seems best. But when we can't agree, we vote, and the majority rules."

"Even the children vote?"

She nodded. "Everyone but the very small babies. So listen carefully and think hard. You may be the one who will solve the problem."

After dinner Racso and Timothy went straight to the meeting room. It was a sea of rats: rats sitting, standing, lying on the floor, chatting, snacking, dozing. There were older rats, babies, and all ages and sizes in between: families, single rats, couples, children playing alone and in groups. It was the first time since the night of their arrival that Racso had seen the entire community in one place, and he was amazed. The room was so packed with rats that it looked to Racso as if not one more could fit through the door.

In the front of the meeting room was a large slate blackboard. And facing the crowd sat Nicodemus, Justin, and Hermione.

Hermione spoke first. "Quiet down! Get ready to think!"

The rats grew still.

Justin stood up. "All of you know that the Trout River, which is fed by the stream and pond outside, has risen almost three feet in the last two months," he said. "We've measured the rainfall as we usually do, and we know that there hasn't been enough rain to cause this kind of flooding. The flooding is being caused by something else."

Justin paused. "We have made three short trips to the Trout in the past two weeks, but so far we haven't been able to find a clue to what's happening."

Hermione turned to the rats for ideas.

"I think we should send scouting parties in both directions along the river for a distance of ten miles," Arthur said. "They should leave early next week and plan to be gone for two full weeks. When they return, we can discuss what they've found and work from there."

Another rat proposed that Arthur and Justin lead the surveillance parties. They agreed to do this, and asked for volunteers to go with them.

"Each party should have six or seven rats in it," Justin said. "They should be rats who like to walk and have keen powers of observation."

Many rats raised their paws to volunteer. Racso and Timothy raised their paws, too. Racso was practically jumping up and down in his eagerness to be chosen.

Justin scanned the room and called out names to Hermione, who wrote them on the blackboard. "Brendan, Sally, Jean, Francis, Max, Brutus, Tom, Becky . . ." He stopped and counted the names.

"I need three more," he said. He looked at the remaining paws.

Racso waved his paw to the right and left, and said, "Me! Me!"

Justin was very deliberate.

"Beatrice and Frank . . ." Justin said. He hesitated, then looked hard at Timothy, whose paw was still in the air. "Are you *sure* you're well enough?"

"I'm sure," Timothy said.

Justin looked at Elvira. "I'll send an extra dose of dried broth, just in case," she said. "But I think he'll do fine."

So Justin added Timothy's name to the list on the blackboard. And that was all.

A few paws remained forlornly in the air, mostly

those of children too young to be chosen. "Next time," Justin said with a smile.

Racso took his paw down. Timothy had been chosen to go on the expedition, but he, Racso, was to stay at home. He began to sulk. He looked in the opposite direction from Timothy with a fixed, hard stare. He hoped that Timothy would notice but, instead, he heard Timothy joking and laughing with Brendan as if he didn't even care.

Racso slunk through the crowd and out the door. He ran down the corridor to his room and flung himself on the bed. They would be sorry! Surely they could have used a rat of Racso's sophistication, a rat who had only recently completed a long and difficult journey. Fools! Fools! Let them find out for themselves what they had missed!

Timothy, Brendan, and Christopher stood in the hallway after the meeting ended.

"Where's Racso?" Brendan asked.

"He left after the scouting parties were chosen," Timothy said. "I think he felt hurt that he wasn't picked."

"I expect Justin wanted rats who could read," Brendan said. "Racso's learning fast, but he couldn't read anything on his own yet."

"I wish I could go," Christopher said. "I didn't even bother to raise my paw. My parents won't let me. They think I'm too wild."

"There's always next time!"

Christopher nodded. "Racso and I will have a good time. There will be plenty to do right here at Thorn Valley."

"Plenty of trouble to get into, you mean," Brendan said, looking at Christopher. "You and Racso should get along just fine."

Christopher smiled. There was a gleam in his eye. But he didn't say anything at all.

Explorers

The rats who had been chosen for the scouting parties met early the following Monday in the conference room. Justin and Arthur stood together with their heads bent over the map.

"My group will travel due south from Thorn Valley until we reach the river about midday tomorrow," Arthur explained. "From there we'll follow the riverbank until the canyon makes it impossible. If we haven't found anything by then, we'll climb the canyon wall and follow it outside the state forest, into human territory."

"We'll head due south along the river," Justin said.

"I expect the terrain there to be wooded, with sloping hills—that's what the crows have said. But no matter what we find, we'll plan to meet you back here at the end of two weeks."

Arthur nodded. "Good luck."

Justin smiled back, but his smile was tense.

The morning was bright and cold. Timothy shivered as he emerged from the tunnel. He had been assigned to Arthur's group, along with Jean, Max, Frank, and Beatrice.

The rats traveled in pairs, with Arthur at the head of the column and Frank bringing up the rear. Timothy's partner was Beatrice, a graceful rat who was known for her adventurousness and for her love of dried mushrooms, which had resulted in the colony's eating mushroom soup, mushroom stew, mushroom bread, and even mushroom pancakes on the days when she worked in the kitchen. She and Timothy trotted side by side with their eyes on Arthur, who might signal them to stop or scatter and hide at any moment.

The first day was easy: They followed the brook that led from Emerald Pond south toward the river. The land was mostly open, with occasional patches of brambles. Arthur checked the sky often for hawks. Before twilight they dug a large hole to sleep in and cut branches to spread over the top for camouflage. Before they went to bed, they ate stalks of wild wheat that grew nearby.

They reached the river in the early afternoon on the second day. The green water was calm and clear, but it had risen so high that its bed included tree trunks and the path that used to follow beside it. Arthur checked the gauge that had been fastened to the trunk of a huge sycamore on his last visit to the river.

"Up another six inches," he told them quietly. He scratched his head in bewilderment. Timothy felt a shiver run down his spine. Were they moving toward danger?

It was almost twilight when they heard the noise. Timothy was the first to be aware of it. He was not sure that he actually heard anything, yet he sensed that there was a sound. He stopped and listened. Again, he *felt* the noise. It reminded him of being in the cinder-block house underground when the tractor was plowing a field close by. There was no sound; but there was a vibration in the air and in the ground that was like sound.

"I feel it, too," Beatrice said, after he had told her. "It reminds me of the feeling of thunder in the sky before you can really hear it."

"Perhaps it's about to storm," suggested Frank.

"We should set up camp well back from the water," Arthur said.

"I'm hungry," Max said. The idea of supper soon had everyone's attention. Max and Timothy found a persimmon tree on the sloping hillside, and when they returned to the others they carried a knapsack stuffed full of the sweet, juicy fruit. Camp had been set up on a knoll protected by shrubbery and pines. From there the rats watched the sun set over the rocky ridge on the opposite side of the valley. Then the moon rose, and they went to sleep.

Timothy was at the river with Arthur the next morning when he heard the sound again. This time the earth itself seemed to tremble ever so slightly beneath his feet. He looked at the surface of the water and saw that it was covered with tiny ripples. He showed Arthur.

"What could it be?"

Arthur shook his head. "I'm not sure." But he looked worried.

The sides of the valley grew steeper as the rats continued south. Around midday they roped themselves together and climbed the cliff. The canyon wall was steep, and when they reached the top, they were exhausted. They lay down on the flat rocks to rest.

Suddenly the cliff shook. A sound like thunder filled the air. The rats leaped to their feet.

"What's *that*?"

Timothy saw Arthur open his mouth to speak, but another explosion followed the first, so that the entire canyon seemed to tremble beneath them. The air was thick with dust. Frank grabbed Timothy and pulled him close as the others huddled in terror. But the blasts stopped as abruptly as they had begun. Once again, the ground was solid underfoot, and the dust settled, so that they could breathe.

"Dynamite," Arthur explained. "It's a powder used by humans to blow holes in the earth. It is very dangerous, although not as powerful as an earthquake or a volcano. It can level a mountainside if they use enough of it."

Timothy's eyes widened. Living on the farm, he had always known that humans were to be feared. Their huge machines could destroy an entire nest of chipmunks or field mice without the driver even knowing what he had done. But to blow holes in the earth, to destroy a mountainside that was home to foxes and hawks and deer mice, was more than he could fathom.

"What are they using it for *here*?" he asked.

Arthur shook his head. "I don't know. But I'd be willing to bet—"

"Wait!" Frank interrupted. "Listen!"

The rats pricked up their ears. The sound they heard now was high-pitched and droning, like a giant insect.

Arthur's legs began to tremble. An expression of terror crossed his face.

"Arthur!" They rushed to his side.

"What is it?" Beatrice whispered. She laid one paw on his shoulder.

"I'd know that sound anywhere," Arthur said in a low voice. "I last heard it the day the humans destroyed the nest under the rosebush at Mr. Fitzgibbon's farm." He breathed deeply, struggling to control his fear. "It's a bulldozer," he said, shivering.

Later that afternoon the rats climbed a rock pinnacle to the highest point of the cliff. From there the scene spread before them like a vast mural: a rock platform covered with men and machines; the river, with a massive barrier stretching halfway across it and a rope bridge connected to the cliffs on the other side; a road running over the mountain down to the edge of the river itself.

"What are they building?" Max asked out loud.
No one answered.

"We should rest," Arthur said. "When it's dark we'll go down and investigate."

It was Beatrice who made the discovery that revealed the secret. The moon was almost full, and the rats could see everything, but still they did not understand. There were the enormous machines: cranes, trucks, bulldozers. They found blasting powder stored in a small, tin-roofed shed. They walked along the concrete wall that channeled most of the river into a narrow passage. Here, to be sure, was the cause of the flooding. Yet for what?

Beatrice slipped away from the group to explore on her own. She discovered an aluminum trailer beside the dirt road that ran up to the mountain pass. It had a door, but this was locked, or at least Beatrice could not open it with her mouth or paws. But one of the windows was slightly ajar. Beatrice wedged her small body into the crack and pushed. She fell, but the fall was broken immediately by the paper-strewn surface of a large desk. It was dark inside the trailer, but Beatrice had good eyes. A thin booklet caught a ray of moonlight from the window, so that its title was illuminated.

Business Plan for the Thorn Valley
Dam and Recreation Center

She read only a few pages before she decided she must fetch Arthur and the others. The small band was just leaving the pontoon bridge. Beatrice walked the last few paces toward them through the darkness with her head down.

"We were *worried*," Arthur scolded; but seeing her expression, he asked quickly, "What have you found?"

"They plan to flood the valley," she said quietly.

There was a moment of silence. Arthur broke it, looking back toward the cement walkway and the rope bridge.

"A dam?" he asked in disbelief.

She nodded.

"Why would they want to build a dam in the middle of the forest?"

"Their plans are in the trailer. I'll show you."

They followed behind Beatrice, slowly, still taking in the news. Timothy stumbled, and an ache started in his side. He had not realized how tired he felt.

Beside him Max spoke through clenched teeth. "We won't let them do it," he whispered fiercely. "We just won't."

Racso at Work

During the days and nights that Timothy was away, Racso was lonely. He felt ashamed that he had lied about his family. He thought about his mother, who went out each night to fetch leftovers from the farmers' market a few blocks away. She always tried to bring back something she thought Racso would particularly like: a few sweet cherries, a raisin, once even the discarded end of a roll of Life Savers with two candies still in it. While she was out, Jenner was nervous. He paced back and forth inside the nest. He was afraid for her, as he was for all of them: afraid that she might be captured, as he had been, years before; afraid that one of the pieces of food she picked up would be bait in a rattrap. He was relieved when she got home. Later in the night, when Racso wanted to go out exploring or to meet friends, Jenner argued. Racso got so sick of the arguments that he often sneaked out without his father's knowing it.

One night he waited until he heard Jenner go to bed, then tiptoed out the door to meet his friends at a dance at the recreation center. The human kids had turned the music up full blast and had flashing lights up on the stage. Racso and the other rats danced in their hiding places behind the baseboard. They shook their shoulders and tails and sang along with the records. Racso was having so much fun that he didn't even think about the time. Then suddenly the record player went off. Racso peeked out. The last teenagers were leaving, and behind them, the janitor. The lock turned in the door.

Racso knew he was in big trouble. The rec center didn't reopen until nine in the morning, and there were no escape routes. When he got home Jenner was waiting for him. Racso thought he would be spanked or at least grounded, but Jenner was too upset to get mad.

"I thought they had caught you." His voice broke. "I thought we'd never see you again."

For once, Racso told the truth about what had happened. He promised himself he would never sneak out again. For a while, he didn't, but then he felt as if he were missing all the fun, so he changed his mind about the promise.

Still, it made Racso feel good, knowing that his father cared so much about him. At Thorn Valley there was no one to ask whether he had eaten all his breakfast, or to tell him to be careful, or to make sure that he went to bed on time. He missed his family.

He missed Timothy, too. He was not sure how he had grown so fond of the little mouse. True, Timothy had saved his life, but that act of courage was not the foundation of their friendship. In fact, Racso felt embarrassed that he had got himself into a situation where he had to be saved at all. Later, when the owl attacked, Timothy had again risked his life for Racso. And yet the times when Racso had felt closest to Timothy began with the days and nights when *he* had cared for Timothy: fed him, told him stories, pulled him in the sling. He had learned then that he, Racso, could help someone.

Since some of the workers were away on the expedition, Nicodemus asked for volunteers to fill in for them. Racso asked to work in the garden and was assigned the job with Christopher under the supervision of an older rat, Bertha.

"I've heard she's *mean*," Christopher whispered.

"Who told you that?"

Christopher grinned. "My cousin. One day she stepped on a pea plant when she was playing tag and Bertha yelled at her. She thinks vegetables are *beau-ti-ful* and children are a nuisance."

Racso was intrigued. In class Christopher was quiet, almost shy. His color was so light that Hermione claimed he blended in with the whitewashed walls, so that she didn't notice him, and when she did call on him he was tongue-tied. But he wasn't tongue-tied now.

Bertha met them by the compost pile on Tuesday afternoon. She had made a list of tasks, neatly printed on a sheet of birch-bark paper, which she handed to Racso. She lectured them on the proper use of garden tools, on the benefits of mulch and compost, and on the life stages of the bean beetle. Racso fidgeted. Christopher kept his eyes on the ground and didn't move. The lecture ended.

"I will meet you back here at four o'clock sharp," she said. "I expect each task on the list to be performed thoroughly and well. The two of you will be working in square Two-B." And she pointed to a small plot behind the blackberry bushes.

Racso cleared his throat. He wanted to tell her that he couldn't read the list, that he was still learning to read; but he was afraid she would be scornful. He handed the paper to Christopher, who studied it long and hard. Bertha eyed them sharply.

"If there are no more questions, I'll be on my way," she said. And she walked away briskly.

"But we never even asked the *first* question," Racso said.

Christopher shrugged. They walked to the garden without looking at each other. Racso saw that it was filled with green, leafy plants about six inches tall.

"What are they?"

"Cabbages?" Christopher suggested.

Racso groaned. "Even I know better than that—cabbages are *round*!"

Christopher scratched behind his ear. "Whatever they are, we have to do the things on this list to them."

Racso didn't want to admit that he couldn't read the list, so he asked Christopher, "Which of the things on the list shall we do first?"

Christopher looked irritated. "The first one, of course." He unfolded the paper and held it out to Racso. "Here!"

Racso drew back his paws as if the paper were a hot potato but Christopher thrust it right under his nose. Racso studied the series of letters without recognizing a single word. He did recognize the letters, and he tried to sound them out in his mind, as Hermione had shown him. But even then he couldn't figure out one word.

"Well," Christopher said, "hurry up! What does it say?"

Racso tried to imagine what it might say, so that he could tell Christopher. Then he thought about Christopher's question. Suddenly he remembered being assigned to study the alphabet with Christopher. Could it be that Christopher couldn't read the list, either? The thought struck him as funny, and he chuckled.

"What's so funny?"

"*You*, that's what!"

Christopher grinned. "I may be funny, but nobody's going to be laughing long if we don't get started on this work. Now, what are we supposed to do first?"

"How would I know?" Racso said lightly. "I can't read."

"But—but . . . I can't read, either!"

"I know," Racso said.

They looked at each other and started to laugh. They laughed harder and harder. Finally, Racso laughed so hard that he fell down. Christopher fell down beside him. They rolled over and over on the soft green plants. Each time they looked at each other, they laughed harder.

Suddenly Christopher stopped laughing. He sat up, and then he stood up. Where he had rolled, the leafy green plants lay crushed against the ground. Racso stood up, too. They looked at the garden and then at each other.

"It's ruined," Christopher said.

Racso couldn't think of what to say. He imagined Bertha returning to the garden to find the plants smashed. Quickly he made a decision.

"We'll have to pick them."

Christopher nodded. They began to work, picking both the leaves and stems of the crushed plants and laying them in a neat pile. The plants gave off a pleasant smell that reminded Racso of something he couldn't quite picture. He ate a leaf, then another.

The taste was sharp and slightly sweet. All at once he realized what it was.

"PEPPERMINT!"

Christopher smiled. "Of course! We use it to make mint tea during the cold weather."

"Tea!" Racso scoffed. "In the city we eat it in candy! Haven't you heard of Peppermint Patties?"

"No," Christopher said.

Racso held his paw out to one side as if he were making a speech. He sang the Peppermint Pattie jingle: "Sweet and gooey, sweet and gooey. Put it in your mouth!" He danced a little dance step, as they did when they sang it on television.

Christopher watched wide-eyed. "I've never tasted candy," he said. "But I've heard that it isn't good for you."

"That's ridiculous! I used to eat it all the time, and look at me!"

Christopher hesitated. "You are a little short for your age."

"That's because I could never get *enough* of it. No, believe me, Christopher, if there's one thing that Thorn Valley needs, it's candy."

"Maybe we could use this mint to make some," Christopher said. "There's a cookbook in the kitchen.

Isabella works there. She could look up the recipe and read it to us."

"Wonderful!" It occurred to Racso that Christopher was really extremely bright. When they had made and served the candy, and he, Racso, was recognized as the one who had brought it to Thorn Valley, he would be sure to let Christopher share in the limelight. After all, Christopher had been present when the idea was first conceived. Racso couldn't wait to get started.

The two rats picked mint for more than an hour. They picked all the plants that had been crushed, and then they picked most of the plants that were still standing. They made two big piles of leaves. After a while the piles were so big that they had to stand up on their hind legs to add more.

Finally all the mint had been picked. Racso looked at the bare ground with satisfaction. He thought about how thrilled the rats would be when they tasted candy for the first time. He decided that it should be a surprise. He would keep them in suspense until it was actually ready. Then he would call to them, "There's a treat for you in the meeting room!" When they tasted it, they would just go crazy!

Racso felt tired. They had been working for a long time. Christopher looked weary, too.

"Let's lie down and rest for five minutes."

Christopher nodded. They curled up together beside the piles of mint. It smelled lovely. The sun had been shining and the ground was comfortably warm. Racso felt very relaxed. He felt his eyes closing. He dreamed about chocolate mints on a wooden platter. He offered a piece to Isabella, who tasted it and smiled at him. She came close to him to give him a kiss. He leaned forward, but someone shrieked right in his ear!

"AUUUUUUUUUUUUGH!"

Racso's eyes flew open, and he leaped to his feet. Christopher stood beside him. Mint leaves were flying into the air, as if someone were trying to knock the pile down from the other side.

There was another scream. Christopher and Racso ran around the pile and saw Bertha standing there. When she saw them she screamed again, "YOU RUINED IT!" She pointed at them with one paw: "YOU! YOU! YOU!"

Rats came running from every direction. Mitchell, the head gardener, hurried up. He looked surprised when he saw the piles of mint and the bare ground where the mint used to be.

"What happened here?" he asked.

Racso remembered the list. He felt nervous. He wanted to say something, but no words came to mind.

"They ruined it," Bertha said in a whisper. Her eyes rolled back in her head, as if she were in shock.

There was a long silence. Racso felt that all eyes were on him. He saw Christopher looking down at his feet. He cleared his throat, but before he could speak, Bertha began to shout:

"I gave them EXPLICIT INSTRUCTIONS! I WROTE IT DOWN!"

Mitchell looked at Racso and Christopher.

Racso fidgeted. He looked hard at his tail, as if it held new interest for him. Finally he spoke, so softly that he could hardly hear his own voice. "We can't read," he said.

Mitchell looked as if he wanted to smile. He scratched his head with his hind leg. Then he gestured to the piles of mint.

"Do you have plans for this?"

Racso could tell that Christopher was too scared to say anything, so he forced himself to speak up.

"Yes," he said. "We want to make a wonderful surprise. It will be something new, and I'm sure you'll all like it a lot."

There was a slight stir among the rats. Someone muttered, "A surprise!" and another rat responded, "I like surprises!" Mitchell looked amused.

"I'm going to tell Nicodemus," Bertha whined. "I'm going to tell him that they ruined my mint patch."

"Our mint patch," Mitchell said, firmly but kindly. "And if it hadn't been picked soon, the cold would have destroyed it anyway."

Bertha snapped her tail against the ground, but she did not say anything. She went and sat by herself behind the blackberry bush.

The remaining rats crowded closer to Racso and Christopher.

"When do we get the surprise?"

"What color is it?"

"Is it bigger than a cabbage? Is it smaller than a peanut?"

Racso smiled. He refused to answer their questions. But when he looked toward the blackberry bush and saw Bertha's lonely silhouette, he felt a little sad. And he resolved to give her the biggest piece of candy.

A Visitor

At the damsite, Timothy and the other rats crept back to the trailer in the dark, sliding one after another through the crack in the window. When all six were inside, they opened the booklets and manuals and began to copy the plans for the dam. They worked by moonlight. But the next night it was cloudy. They lit beeswax candles and covered the window of the trailer with a workman's jacket they found hanging on the door.

They realized that the dam was a life-and-death matter and that the lake it would create would flood not just their colony but the entire valley. And they had no way of knowing how fast the humans could work.

"Until we know what their plans are," Arthur said, "we won't be able to fight back."

"If we're in the meeting room at night when the flooding begins," Frank said, "we'll be trapped in there, and we'll never escape alive."

"Like drowned rats," Beatrice said quietly. "Isn't that the expression they use?"

"Stop talking about it," said Max.

But even when they did stop talking about it, Timothy could not stop himself from thinking about it. He imagined that the dark waters of the flood were already lapping at the sides of the trailer where they crouched, and climbing slowly higher and higher. He strained to work faster, faster; his pen fairly flew across the paper.

All of them were tired. They tried to sleep during the day, but it was hard. The area around the dam was noisy and shook constantly from the explosions in the cliff. There was not enough cover for them to stay together, so they had to separate into small groups: Timothy and Beatrice in one thicket; Arthur and Max in another; Jean and Frank in a large crack in the rocky cliff. The dust got in their eyes and in their food. They ate only what they could gather—

roots, twigs, the inner parts of the leathery cactus plants that grew along the canyon wall. No one said so, but all were looking forward to the last night when the two weeks would be almost over and they would go home.

When the sun rose on the twelfth day, they set out immediately, without waiting to rest. They were a ragtag bunch, dirty and tired, their knapsacks heavy with papers, their stomachs growling. Slowly, as they moved farther and farther from the damsite, Timothy felt his body begin to relax. That night he slept well. The dangers of the dam were in the future. For tonight, there was a comfort in the six tired bodies under the same roof of brush and shrub. They had, at least, each other.

The next morning, over a breakfast of hickory nuts, they talked about what to tell the rats at home.

"Shall we tell everyone at once?"

"I think it would be better for each of us to speak to a group of fifteen or twenty rats," Arthur said. "That way we'll have time to answer everyone's questions as well as we can. We can speak then of the need to devise a plan."

"It will come down to a choice," said Beatrice. "Leaving or fighting."

They nodded. The nuts were gone. They scattered the empty shells among the fallen leaves and continued the journey home.

Racso and Christopher heard the news directly from Timothy. They climbed a tree after school got out on the day the surveillance parties were expected home. They were the first to see Justin's group, marching in orderly fashion from the south, and they screamed greetings from their perch on an overhanging branch:

"WELCOME BACK! DID YOU FIND ANYTHING?"

Justin waved, they all waved, but they shook their heads no.

Arthur's group arrived two hours later, walking slowly along the north bank of the stream. Racso and Christopher spied them from their lookout on the tree branch. They raced down the trunk and scurried across a fallen tree that bridged the creek.

"Timothy!" Racso shouted. "Welcome home! Did you have a good time? Christopher and I are planning a surprise! Did you find out why the river's flooded?"

When Racso heard about the dam—for Timothy described the journey bit by bit: the vibrations, the dust, the men shouting, the machines, and, finally, Beatrice's discovery of the plans—his eyes got big and round. His whiskers drooped. He sat bolt upright without speaking. Christopher and Timothy didn't notice anything unusual for a moment, until Christopher bumped Racso by accident. Racso didn't blink.

"Timothy!" Christopher said. "Look at this!" He touched Racso's nose, his paws, his tail, but there was no response.

"Racso!" Timothy exclaimed. He grasped Racso's shoulders and gave them a hard shake. But Racso was as still as a statue.

"What's wrong with him?"

"I don't know," Timothy said. "Maybe you'd better go fetch Elvira."

Elvira didn't hesitate to make a diagnosis. "Paralyzed by fear," she said curtly. "A little horseradish broth should bring him out of it. I'll get Brutus to carry him down to the infirmary, and I'll pour a bit of it down his throat. He'll be alive and kicking in no time."

Later Racso was indignant. He rinsed his mouth out five times, but the bitter taste persisted. "You could have given me tea and honey," he pouted to Elvira. "That's what my mother would have done."

"But I'm not your mother," Elvira said, smiling as though she might be glad that were the case.

"You're not a good doctor, either, torturing your patients with stuff like that," Racso said. "I could do better than that myself."

Elvira stood with her back to Racso. She lit a fire under a little beaker of brown stuff and stirred it with a rod.

"I'm in the process of developing some new remedies," she said. "If you like, I'll let you do a little experiment."

"What is it?"

"I'll let you taste them all, and you can tell me which is the most bitter."

"Very funny." Racso smacked his tail down hard on the floor of the laboratory.

Elvira looked around. "I'd be careful with that tail if I were you," she said. "You could crack one of the vestigial vertebrae. Then I'd have to put a tail brace on you. And those can be awfully cumbersome." She smiled.

When Racso left the infirmary he was too mad to be scared anymore.

*　　*　　*

Arthur, Beatrice, Justin, Hermione, and Nicodemus studied the pages copied from the planning
manual for four days. Much of the language from
the book was technical, and there were parts that
even Arthur, who had studied engineering, could
not understand. But the overall plan was clear.

"What *I* don't understand," said Justin, "is how
they can do it. The state forest is supposed to be
preserved forever, by law. That's one of the reasons
we moved here."

Arthur shrugged. "It may not be legal. But whether
it is or not, they're doing it—we saw them with our
own eyes."

"But why? *Why* are they willing to take that risk?"

"Money. If the dam is built, tourists will flock to
see the lake, and tourists mean money."

"But the farmers will fight it," Justin argued.
"They've been on that land for generations."

"It will be hard for the farmers. To fight the dam
legally will take time and money, and the farmers
don't have much of either."

"Then it's hopeless." Justin's shoulders slumped.

"No." Nicodemus stepped in now. "It is *not* hopeless."

A Visitor

The rats paused to eat some acorns and roasted sunflower seeds. It was hard for Justin to sit still. Although he was thoughtful and deliberate, he liked to take action. When he heard of a threat, the fur stood up on the back of his neck, and his heart beat faster. He knew, of course, that they had to be rational, to figure out a plan and to act on it. But it was hard to think about fighting an enemy made of steel and concrete, with a mechanized brain.

Beatrice sat beside him, eating quietly. She appeared unruffled by the thought of what was to come. Justin admired her. She was dogged and delicate at once, courageous and considerate. He was not sure why he had not noticed that before. He offered her the bowl of acorns, and his paw brushed the soft gray fur of her neck. He liked the way it felt. She smiled and thanked him as she took more.

They had just returned to study the plans when there was a knock on the door and Brutus burst in. He sounded out of breath, as if he had been running.

"A crow with a mouse on its back!" he shouted. "I just saw it! It came from the sky!"

"Where?" The others got to their feet.

"By Emerald Pond. I was fishing, and I looked up and saw them. They didn't see me—I hid behind the reeds!"

"Calm down," Hermione told Brutus gently. She glanced at Nicodemus.

"You go investigate," he said. "Send me word of what you find."

It was only a minute before the group, led by Justin, had skipped across the garden path, over the bridge, and through the tall grass that surrounded the pond. From a clearing near the water's edge they could see directly across the pond to the spot where a huge crow was standing ankle-deep in the green water. A small brown field mouse, a shawl across her shoulders, still clung tightly to his feathers. She was wet.

"But I *always* land here," Jeremy protested, in a rasping voice. "A little water never hurt anyone."

The mouse replied in a voice too low to be heard across the water.

"Don't worry," the crow resumed. "They'll find us."

"Mrs. Frisby," Justin said kindly. "It's wonderful to see you."

"I'm glad to be here," she answered politely. Arthur helped her down off the crow and brought her a dry leaf to wipe the water from her face.

"I've brought news from the farm," she said. "And I'm afraid it's bad." Her voice faltered and she was trembling. "Nicodemus wrote me that Timothy is here, and well," she continued. "I'd like to see him."

"Of course," Justin said. And he sent Brutus to the schoolroom. "He's just fine," he told Mrs. Frisby. "He really is."

Decisions

Mrs. Frisby sat holding Timothy's paw as if she could not let it go. "For three days I thought he was dead," she told them.

"We wrote you," Justin said.

She nodded. "The winds were strong the night the courier came. The packet dropped far south of our house, in a thicket along the fencerow, and the letter wasn't found until several days after you sent it."

"It must have been terrible for you," Nicodemus said softly.

Mrs. Frisby did not answer, but her eyes filled with tears.

Hermione decided to call a general meeting while Mrs. Frisby and Jeremy were at Thorn Valley, so that they could be part of the discussion about the dam. The meeting was held in the pine grove near the brook. It was cold outdoors, but Jeremy was too big to fit inside the rats' nest, so the rats brought reed mats to sit on and wrapped their babies in scraps of cloth. Brendan and Christopher had dragged the slate blackboard out of the classroom and propped it against a tree trunk, and the rats sat facing this, with Mrs. Frisby in the front row and Jeremy in the back.

Hermione summarized the news in a loud, clear voice.

"By now you all know what Arthur's group discovered at the northern end of Thorn Valley. Men have begun work on a dam to block off the Trout River. The dam will be operated by a computer and will create a deep lake in the valley, flooding our home and the homes of animals who live near us. The farms that lie just outside the state forest will be taken over by the state for highways, motels, and campgrounds. This means that old friends like Mrs. Frisby will also be forced to move." Hermione paused. The rats were silent, grim. She looked at them and forced herself to smile.

"One thing in our favor is this," she said. "Concrete, which forms the main wall of the dam, will not set in freezing weather. We can be sure that the remaining work on the dam will not be completed until spring. That means the water will not rise any higher than it is now. So the danger to us is not immediate." She flipped through the pages of a hand-lettered calendar, then held it up for all the rats to see. "They hope to open the dam in the late spring. Today is the eighteenth of November. So we have six months.

"We have faced crises before, and we have found solutions," Hermione said finally. "A dam is a big problem, and we are small. But being small, and smart, has its advantages. We can move quickly and hide ourselves easily. And an unknown enemy is hard to fight."

Hermione asked Mrs. Frisby to come forward, and the small mouse did so.

"Tell them what you know, Mrs. Frisby," Hermione said gently.

"I don't think I can," Mrs. Frisby whispered. Her

throat felt completely dry. Yet when she looked at Timothy, sitting beside Racso and Christopher in the front row, she knew that she could speak, and that she must.

"It began one evening when I noticed a stream of cars and trucks pulling into the Fitzgibbons' driveway," Mrs. Frisby said. "At first I thought there must be a party, the way there is every Christmas. But people were standing around in the yard talking seriously. I recognized the Simmons family from down the road, and the Hanson boys—they were carrying chairs into the barn. No one was laughing, and for some reason that made me feel nervous. I decided I had better find out what was going on.

"It wasn't as easy to get to the barn as it usually is. I checked first for the cat, then sneaked along the fencerow until I came to the crack in the side of the barn. There were a lot of people in the barn—forty, at least. I could tell by their clothes that most of them were farmers. I scurried up on the big beam, where I could get a clear view of what was happening.

"A stranger in a suit called the meeting to order. He introduced himself as Representative Jones, from the state legislature. He showed the farmers maps of where the dam and lake would be. He said they would be well paid for their land, which would be turned into campgrounds and motels for tourists."

Mrs. Frisby paused. "That was when the shouting began. I was so shocked by the news that I was in a daze for a few moments, so I didn't hear everything they said. I kept thinking, What about us? What about the animals? The farmers were yelling about their land, saying that they didn't want to sell it, and they didn't want the dam or the lake, that it was being forced down their throats. There was a newspaper reporter there, too. Her name was Lindsey Scott, and she had red hair and glasses. I remember that she asked about what would happen to the wildlife in the valley. And later she asked another question that made Representative Jones very angry. It was something about his cousin's construction company, which was working at the damsite."

There was a murmur of approval for Mrs. Frisby as she returned to her seat. Hermione nodded to Jeremy. She thanked him for bringing Mrs. Frisby to the valley.

"I know that you are a bold explorer and are known among the rest of the crows for your keen eyesight," she said. This was flattery, for, in fact, Jeremy was not one of the more quick-witted or observant crows.

But the rats could see from the gleam in his yellow eyes that he was pleased.

"Have you visited the damsite?" Hermione asked.

Jeremy squawked yes. "The men throw away their breadcrusts," he said. "They taste good!"

"How long does it take to fly there from here?"

"It's an easy flight," Jeremy said with enthusiasm. "If the wind is right, it takes only an hour."

"Do you think you could help us by flying some of us there, or by carrying messages back and forth for us?"

"I know I could, if my mother will let me. She told me not to go there anymore. That's where she broke her wing. The humans made a big bang, and rocks and dirt flew into the sky where she was flying. For a moment, she was blinded. She flew into a ladder on a big truck. She said she's lucky to be alive. But I want to help!" Jeremy exclaimed loudly. "I want to save the valley!"

"I know," Hermione said softly. "We all want that. I'll send word to your mother."

Next Hermione stepped up to the blackboard and wrote in large letters:

OUR OPTIONS
1. Leave the valley and find a new home

2. Wait and see what happens
3. Fight the dam

For a moment there was silence as the rats considered their situation. Then there were whispers, then the buzz of excited conversation.

Nolan was the first to speak. "I don't know where we'd move this time."

"We've done so much to build a home here," Beatrice said. "I'd hate to abandon the valley after all those days of planning and hard work. But I think we can build a new home if we have to."

"But should we?" Arthur asked.

Answers—and more questions—began to explode from the crowd.

"Yes!"

"No!"

"How can we fight something like this? It involves hundreds of people!"

"There are a hundred of us—more than a hundred!"

"But we're not as important as people!"

"We are, too! And they have no right to harm us, or the other animals that live in Thorn Valley."

"They're making people move, too," Justin pointed out.

"Could we work with the farmers who are fighting the dam?"

"No, they'd kill us—or worse, put us back in the laboratory!"

"Not if we helped them win this battle."

"What could we do?"

The rats thought for some time. Finally, Christopher piped up: "We could drill little holes in the dam."

"They'd fill them in," Isabella said.

"We could pretend to have rabies," Brendan suggested. "Then the workers might refuse to go there to fix the dam."

"I think they'll fix the dam eventually, no matter what we do to it," Justin said. "Breaking the dam is a good idea, but we have to do more than that."

More than that . . . Racso only half heard what Justin was saying. Ever since Hermione had mentioned the computer, he had been daydreaming. *He* had seen a computer once. He remembered it vividly. He had been lost that night, wandering through tunnels in the walls of a huge office building where he had heard that humans kept a large supply of potato chips and candy. Another rat had given him directions to a room he called the canteen, where the candy lay open in boxes. But somewhere in the maze of passageways he had taken a wrong turn.

Then, through the tunnel wall, he heard a noise. He froze, thinking at first that it was the security man making his late-night rounds; but the noise continued for a long time. It was not a radio or TV, Racso knew at once, for there were no voices, and although it was a pleasant sound, he was sure it was not music. It was a gentle, beeping sound, which reminded Racso of water dripping from a faucet.

Finally, as the noise continued in a rhythmic pattern, Racso crept to a crack in the baseboard and looked through. He saw a small room that was filled with a large machine. The machine had a gray surface like a table, but this table was covered with buttons and switches and looked like a typewriter. On top of the table were three screens, which were lit up with flashing lines and emitted the beeping sounds.

There was no one in the room. Racso stayed behind the baseboard for a long time, listening and watching. He decided that he wanted to touch the machine. Slowly, with ever so much caution, he squeezed out of the crack. No one came. He walked across the floor to the machine and ran up one of the legs, so that he was standing just below the keyboard. The screens flashed on and off, as before. From where he stood he could see that each switch was marked with what seemed to be a letter or a number. Racso knew that the next thing he did was foolish. He wanted to do it, and he wanted not to do it because he knew he should not. A button clicked under his front paw. But nothing happened. The screens continued to light up and make the same soft, beeping noise.

He pushed another switch. Still, nothing changed. He began to feel a little more confident. He began to push buttons with both front paws, one after another; and then he began to push the buttons with all four feet. He was practically dancing on the keyboard. Click, click, click went the buttons. The machine continued to beep. Then something changed; it beeped faster, and all of a sudden it made a screaming sound. Racso leaped for the crack. He heard human feet running in the hallway. He tore through the tunnels at top speed, finally finding, with relief, a hole that led back into the sewer system.

"You are a very foolish young rat," his father had

said sternly. "You set off the alarm on the computer system. You could have been caught, and they would have killed you."

"I had to do it," Racso said.

"I have to do this," Jenner replied. And he had spanked Racso.

OUCH! The memory of *that* made Racso shake his head. And when he shook his head, it was as if the pieces of a puzzle suddenly came together. He didn't wait to raise his paw. He just blurted it out.

"We'll program the computer!" he shouted. "We'll program it to destroy the dam!"

Everyone stared.

"And we'll make it wreck itself afterward, so they can't use it again!"

Arthur scratched his head. "It would wipe out everything they've done."

"And it would look like their mistake," Beatrice said. "As if they didn't know what they were doing. They'd have no one else to blame!"

"But could we do it?" Justin's voice was measured, hopeful. "After all, what do we know about computers?"

"We could learn," Sally said.

Nicodemus nodded. "We'll write our own program," he said. "It may be hard, but I think we can do it."

"I think so, too!" Beatrice was on her feet, ready to begin.

One by one the rats agreed. Their doubts turned to resolve: "We will do it!"

Racso grinned from ear to ear. "I'll bet *I* could write the program," he said.

Most of the rats smiled, but Isabella looked disgusted. "Sure—you and Albert Einstein." She got up to leave.

Racso was tolerant. "Wait and see." His gaze followed her as she pushed through the crowd and made her way back toward the entrance hole. She was, after all, a very attractive rat.

To Beat the Computer

There was so much to be done! The rats met twice
more while Mrs. Frisby was with them. Together
they made three decisions. The first was that they
must learn as much about computers as they could.
The second was that a group of rats must enter a
special training program for the assault on the dam;
from this group, a smaller number would be chosen
to perform the actual mission. The third was that
the remainder of the colony would be evacuated to
a safe place just before the opening of the dam. They
would carry with them only tools and seeds, for they

hoped to return to the nest in Thorn Valley after the mission.

They enlisted the help of their trusted allies, Mrs. Frisby and Jeremy, in the struggle. From them, they would learn as much as possible about the farmers' plan of resistance. Nicodemus would mail letters to the largest computer companies for up-to-date information and have it sent to the address of a vacant farmhouse down the road from the Fitzgibbons. Jeremy could pick up the replies from the mailbox and fly them directly to Thorn Valley.

Justin was in charge of the training program, which was held in the mornings before breakfast and in the evenings after school or work. Forty rats signed up for the sessions, but Justin made it clear that only fifteen would be chosen for the final mission.

"Try not to be disappointed if you're one of those who is asked to stay here," he said. "Remember that the evacuation of Thorn Valley is work just as vital to our survival as the mission itself."

The young rats nodded. Still, Racso was sure that he would be chosen. After all, he had thought up the idea. And during the training sessions Justin would have a good chance to observe his prowess.

Not only that, but wait until Justin and the others tasted the candy! He would be a hero, after all. Soon even Nicodemus would have to say so.

Racso looked around. By now he knew all the other rats by name: Brendan, Sally, Christopher, Nolan, Beatrice, Brutus. Timothy was here, of course, and next to him was Isabella. She had chosen a seat directly in front of Justin. Each time Justin glanced in her direction, she smiled and flitted her eyes at him. Justin pretended not to notice. Racso wished Isabella would flit her eyes at *him*.

The training was hard. In the mornings the rats ran the entire distance between Emerald Pond and the lower part of the mountain trail. They practiced digging tunnels, climbing steep rocks, and running one by one through an obstacle course. They practiced diving for cover on command, and not coming out until Justin blew the whistle that meant "all clear."

In the evenings Arthur lectured them about computers. He loved machines, and his enthusiasm was infectious. The young rats were incredulous as Arthur described tiny chips of silicon that could hold thousands of pieces of information.

"When we were captives in Dr. Schultz's laboratory, the scientists shared a computer in a room just down the hall from us," he said. "We used to let ourselves out at night and go look at it. It was big—almost as big as a piano. Today that same computer's memory could be stored in a space as small as the surface of a pebble."

Next Arthur drew a picture of a computer on the blackboard, and he labeled its parts: the terminal, the keyboard, the viewing screen, the disk drive. "The computer plays the disk in the same way that a phonograph plays a record," he explained. "The disk has instructions on it, and the set of instructions is called a program."

"Who will program the computer that runs the dam?" Christopher asked.

"The humans have probably developed their program already," Arthur said. "I expect it will be at the damsite when we arrive, stored in a special file. We will use their program to create ours. On the night before the dam is to open we plan to erase their program and substitute ours on the same disks."

In December Racso got into trouble. It started when he gave Christopher a really wonderful Christmas present. He found out later that the rats weren't in the habit of giving Christmas presents. But how could he have known that? Timothy said, "You could have asked me." But Racso scowled and looked the other way. What good was a suggestion that came too late?

The present was a purple headband covered with glitter. The glitter came from chips of mica that Racso had carefully picked off a rock beside the creek. The headband itself was made of birch-bark paper he had painted purple one day at school. Racso pasted the shiny chips on one by one. He tried the headband on himself, using the pond as his mirror. It was great! Racso thought he looked like a rock star he had seen on TV back in the city. He tried swinging his hips and singing the lyrics to the star's latest hit, "Sweet Lorinda," in a falsetto voice. He hated to give the headband up, but he did, and he congratulated himself on being so generous.

The problem happened because Christopher liked the present too much. He wanted to wear the headband all the time. He went around singing the lyrics of "Sweet Lorinda" under his breath, so that he couldn't hear what anyone said to him. Sometimes he wouldn't even answer Racso!

Then Sally made herself a glitter headband. She looked a lot more glamorous than Christopher, and she had a higher, sweeter voice when she sang "Sweet Lorinda." Christopher had learned to swing his hips the way Racso had shown him, and he could shuffle all four paws in a dance that was a pretty good imitation of a real star. When it was his turn to recite his lessons, he danced and sang instead. Then Sally wanted to sing, too. Hermione tried to be tolerant, but she had some misgivings about the way things were going. Most of the students were still trying to learn their lessons, but the atmosphere in the classroom seemed different.

Racso realized later that he should have waited longer with his next idea. It was an old trick, of course, but before he had learned how to read he hadn't been able to do it. He explained it to Timothy one night in their bedroom.

"All you do is reverse the order of the letters. Then you sound them out. And it's like a secret language."

"Wow!" Timothy grinned. "That's neat."

"My old man showed me how. . . . He did it on my name. I liked the way it sounded so much that after that I never wanted to be called anything else."

"Let's see . . ." Timothy bent over a piece of paper. "R-A-C-S-O. Then I turn them around: O-S-C-A-R. Oscar! Is that your real name?"

Racso chuckled. "It was. But I changed it officially

when I ran away from home. Oscar sounds like a sissy, but Racso sounds tough!"

"Let's see what my name would be." Timothy scribbled the letters, then changed them around. "Yhtomit! Sounds like a guy from outer space, doesn't it?"

"Or some kind of monster." Racso smiled. "Want me to call you that?"

"Sure."

At first Timothy and Racso just used the backward language in their bedroom, or when they wanted to share a special secret. But then Timothy told Brendan, who became Nadnerb, and the next day Yllas and Rehpotsirhc joined the club. Then they began to say "sey" and "on" instead of yes and no, and "Yellav Nroht" instead of Thorn Valley. They called Justin "Nitsuj" and answered "tneserp" when he called the roll during the training sessions, until after a few days he got irritated and told them to cut it out.

They used the code in the schoolroom, too. Racso's favorite stunt was to throw in a few backward phrases when he was giving a report in front of the whole class. That way all the students would grab their pens and start writing down whatever he had said, to try to figure out what it meant. Racso thought it was a good way to learn spelling, but Hermione disagreed. Her patience was wearing thin. She decided to go to Nicodemus for advice.

It was about that same time that Brendan figured something out. They were sitting in the cafeteria with Christopher and Timothy when he asked Racso, "Where did you learn about the backward code?"

"My father showed me. But since I didn't know how to read and write, I couldn't do it. He had to help me."

"Who taught your father how to read?"

Racso gulped. Suddenly the conversation had become dangerous. "There's a tutor at the mansion, and my old man overheard him teaching the kids. So he picked it up there."

Brendan was dubious. He seemed to be thinking out loud. "It's quite a coincidence that you turned up at Thorn Valley, the only *other* place in the world where rats can read and write. Not only that, but Thorn Valley is a secret. Rats outside the valley don't know about it."

"Some do," Racso said weakly. "My father did."

"He might have had some connection with Nimh in the past," Brendan continued. "The rats in the laboratory got special shots that made them smart.

There's no evidence that an ordinary rat could have learned to read."

"He did!" Racso felt as if he were entering a trap, as if the steel gates were going to slam behind him at any moment. He looked at Timothy for help, but Timothy looked away.

Even Christopher had stopped singing and was interested in what Brendan was saying. "Maybe your dad *was* at Nimh," he suggested. "Maybe he just never told you about it."

Before Racso could answer, Brendan said, "All the rats who escaped—those who had gotten the special shots, that is—stayed together, along with Jonathan Frisby and Mr. Ages. Some of the mice did get swept away in the air ducts, but everyone else traveled as a group until they finally settled under the rosebush at the Fitzgibbons' farm. And then they stayed together until just before the move to Thorn Valley. I remember that in the history—"

"Maybe your father is really a mouse," Christopher conjectured. "Maybe he found his way out of the air ducts and—"

"That would explain why you're so short!" Brendan smiled sweetly.

Racso was scared and furious at the same time.

[148]

"He's not a mouse! And stop making up stories about him! Stop talking about it!"

Brendan seemed genuinely surprised at Racso's outburst. "You act as if you're trying to hide something."

"I'm not!" Racso stared at the carrots in his bowl. He had lost his appetite. Brendan and Christopher—Christopher, to whom he had given the headband!—had almost figured out about Jenner.

A Bargain Struck

When Nicodemus asked to speak with him, Racso actually felt relieved. He was not surprised that Nicodemus had some comments about the headbands and the backward code language.

"It's not that there's anything *wrong* with them," Nicodemus said. "It's just that there isn't that much right with them, either. How much good does a rock star do? Do rock stars really make the world a better place?"

"They're fun."

"Other things are fun, too."

"I know." Racso tried to keep the disgust out of

his voice. "Like gardening, and square dancing, and playing hide-and-seek. And eating your fresh vegetables. And being a good little rat."

Nicodemus raised his eyebrows.

"And some of the rats around here are losing their sense of humor, if you ask me," Racso said darkly.

"It's hard to be lighthearted in a crisis."

"I'm in trouble, too." Racso let the words slide out fast so that he couldn't take them back.

"What about?"

"Lying. And Jenner."

"What do you want me to do about it?"

Racso's voice was weak. "Help me."

"Advice?"

Racso nodded.

Nicodemus paused, as if he were making a deliberate calculation. When he spoke, he sounded businesslike. "All right. But the advice will cost you something."

"What do you mean?"

"I'll give you advice . . . but before I do, you'll have to agree to this: to give up rock stars and code language for the rest of the winter, until the sabotage unit leaves."

"But that's blackmail!" Racso was indignant.

Nicodemus shrugged.

Racso pushed his lips together hard. He really needed advice, but he'd never thought that Nicodemus would pull a trick like this. On the other hand, what if Brendan figured out that Jenner was Racso's father and that he'd been lying about it the whole time? He'd feel so humiliated he wouldn't be able to stay. He was stuck.

Nicodemus seemed to sense what he was feeling. He looked sympathetic. "Look, Racso," he explained, "these are troublesome times for us. With the dam crisis hanging over our heads, everyone is scared. We don't know what will happen or where we'll be six months from now. There's a danger that we could lose our direction, and if that happens, the mission will fail." Nicodemus paused. "I have to do whatever I can to keep the community united until the crisis is over. And I need your help."

Racso was pleased to be asked to help. "Okay," he said, "no more code until Thorn Valley is saved." He sighed deeply.

"Thank you," said Nicodemus. "Now what's this about lying and Jenner?"

"You remember I didn't want the others to know about Jenner? So I told them my father lives in a mansion and learned to read from the children's tutor there. But Brendan said an ordinary rat couldn't have learned to read, and that my father must have been at the laboratory . . . so I'm afraid they're going to figure it out."

"And what if they do?"

"They'll hate me for what he did. And they'll make fun of me for wanting to be a hero, because my old man was—" Racso's voice seemed to give out suddenly.

"I would say he was a rebel," Nicodemus said softly.

Racso thought of Jenner—scarred, bitter, and lonely.

"I don't want to lie about him, but I can't stand to tell the truth, either," he admitted.

"Why not?"

"They'll think it served him right, what happened to him."

Nicodemus leaned his head against one paw thoughtfully. "Why don't you tell them that you lied about your father living in the mansion, but that you had your own reasons for doing so. And ask them not to ask you more about it until you're ready to say more."

Racso was surprised. The advice would be difficult to follow, but he thought he could do it. "Thank you," he said, relieved.

"I'm going for a walk in the garden," Nicodemus said. "Would you like to come with me?"

Racso nodded.

They walked along a stone walkway bordered with glossy rhododendron. The walkway was overhung by taller plants and trees, and the effect, even in winter, was lovely and peaceful. Racso had heard from Timothy that gardening was Nicodemus's hobby, but the older rat did not mention this. The walkway led into a small pine grove. Beyond the trees was a clear, fast-flowing brook. To one side Racso noticed a mossy bank with a small gray stone on it. The stone was a rectangle about six inches high, with quartz crystals embedded along the sides. Racso stared at it. They approached the stone and stood in front of it. Racso saw that it had been engraved with the letter "R."

"That's the first letter of my name," he said.

Nicodemus smiled. "I remember that I told you we want Thorn Valley to be a place where heroes are unnecessary. But the truth is that we haven't reached that point. The move from Mr. Fitzgibbon's farm was a trial for us—for some, a test of faith; for others, a test of physical endurance. Two rats gave their lives so that we could make that move. This is a memorial to them."

They stood for a moment in silence. Then Racso asked, "Who were they?"

"One was a rat called Martha, who had come with us from Nimh. She had tremendous strength and cunning and was almost fearless. She was older than most of us and had fought on the streets before she ever got to the laboratory. She volunteered to be part of the last guard—the rats who stayed to trick the humans into believing that they had destroyed an ordinary rats' nest."

"And the other?"

"The truth is that we don't really know," Nicodemus said sadly. "He was a large, reddish rat who simply appeared on our doorstep at Mr. Fitzgibbon's farm in late winter, about a month before the move. He was practically starving. We gave him food and sent him away, but he kept coming back—he said he wanted to pay us back for helping him out. Eventually we let him stay. He was different from us. He was not bright, even for a normal rat, and he never understood why we had decided to leave our nest. We tried to teach him letters, and he tried to learn, but 'R'—for 'Red'—was the only letter he ever recognized. But what a worker! I don't know if we would have been ready to move if it hadn't been for him. He could move one pound of seed in a single carry, and he worked around the clock.

"The day came when the colony left for Thorn Valley. Nine of us stayed to destroy the nest. Red came back that night. 'I want to help,' he said.

"We knew the end would be dangerous: Mrs. Frisby had overheard that Dr. Schultz from Nimh planned to gas the nest, to collect specimens. He suspected that some of us were the rats of Nimh. At dawn we heard the tractor start. They must have put a bull-dozer blade on it, because we saw the roots of the rosebush fly up into the air. There was a terrible stench. I ran behind the others, toward the hidden door. I could see the sky when Justin stopped me. 'We're missing two!' Red never spoke, he just turned around and went back in. I came out, gasping. After the others had stopped circling and dodging, I counted seven. Later Brutus was pushed out. Red had saved him, and gone back for Martha."

They stood for a moment in silence. A question plagued Racso. Finally he asked, "Why did he do it?"

"I don't know. I've thought about it a lot. We've never been able to find his family or even where he came from. We never even got his body—the doctor took that, and Martha's too. That's one of the reasons we put up this stone."

"The 'R,' " said Racso. "Does it stand for Red?"

"It stands for Rat," Nicodemus said. "It's for him and for Martha, and for other rats who work or die for what they believe in."

Racso looked at Nicodemus quickly. "For what they believe in," he had said. Racso realized suddenly that Nicodemus loved the colony: loved it so much that he had risked his life for it; so much that he would do almost anything to protect it from the world outside.

Racso thought about himself. He had longed to learn to read and write, so that he could become a scientist and do experiments. He wanted to be successful and famous. He also wanted to be serious, to accomplish things that were important, that he cared about and could be proud of.

Nicodemus seemed to read his mind. "Last week Elvira came to talk with me," he said. "She's looking for an assistant to work in the lab with her, starting next summer. I knew you were interested in science, so I mentioned your name. She wasn't very enthusiastic at first, but after we talked a little longer she thought it might work out." He chuckled. "I think you two could get along if you tried."

"Oh!" Racso was thrilled and terrified. To work in the lab and do experiments! But to work with

Elvira, who had the worst temper of any rat in the valley—except, perhaps, for Isabella! He struggled to keep his composure.

"I think I'd like that," he said. "I'm sure I could help Elvira. I've sampled children's vitamins and cough drops in drugstores all over the city. I know all the best flavors and what they're made from. Medicine doesn't have to be bitter, you know."

Nicodemus had turned his back, as if he hadn't even heard what Racso said. "Isn't that the training unit lining up over there?"

"I'm late!" And Racso was off, in a flurry of legs and tail.

The Basket

January came to the valley. There was a thick frost on the ground. It was hard for the rats in the training unit to keep from shivering as each one approached Justin and was handed a folded piece of paper.

Racso sounded out the words the best he could.

Special Assignment: Racso
   You are to make a map of the south side of the creek to the large walnut tree on the bank approximately one mile to the east. Include any landmarks. Be back by noon.
Your Partner Is: Isabella

Racso was pleased that he could read most of the assignment, and when he got to the word "Isabella," he was overjoyed! When he found her, Isabella had just finished tying some vines onto a wicker basket so that she could wear it on her back like a knapsack.

Racso pulled his beret down over his ears. "We're going together, you know. You and me."

She glared. "How could I forget?"

Racso decided to be a gentleman. His manners would win her over.

"I've got my pen and some paper. Do we need anything else?"

"You could use a few more inches, if you ask me."

He ignored the remark and put on his knapsack.

Justin approached the two of them. "What's this? You haven't left yet?"

"We're just going now," Isabella said in a nicer tone of voice.

"Why are you taking that produce basket? Isn't that going to be clumsy in the brush?"

Isabella smiled sweetly. "I'm in charge of dinner tonight, and I thought I might find some persimmons near the creek. Persimmons are one of your favorites, aren't they, Justin?"

Justin ignored the question. "Run along, now,"

he said. "Don't forget to blow the emergency whistle if you get into trouble. And try not to be late."

And so they went together. Racso hummed a cheerful tune as he led the way, with Isabella following sullenly. There was a path along the south side of the pond, but beyond that the brush grew thick and they had to bushwhack their way through, pushing their shoulders hard against the wiry branches. The creek flowed swiftly beside them. It was clear and deep. In some spots the water formed waves, with frothy whitecaps along the tops. Racso liked the way it looked, but he couldn't forget the time he had tried to go swimming on his way to Thorn Valley and had almost drowned.

They spotted the walnut tree after a twenty-minute walk. There were still a few lonely walnuts hanging on its bare limbs. Racso wanted to throw stones at them and knock them down, but Isabella said there was no time for that, and she made Racso take the pen and paper out of his knapsack. He made a mark at the far end of the paper to represent the tree.

"You should write the words 'walnut tree,' " Isabella pointed out. "Otherwise, that could be any tree on the south side of the creek."

She was right. Racso laboriously printed the letters: w-a-l-n-u. Then he came to the end of the page. The letters were too big.

Isabella was exasperated. "Let *me* do it." She took another piece of paper, drew the tree, and wrote under it, in prim script, "walnut tree." She drew perpendicular lines to represent the banks of the creek close to the tree. Racso watched carefully.

They pushed their way through the brambles to get closer to the shoreline. There was a small, sandy beach just below them. But as they began to descend toward it, they heard a grating sound.

"What was that?" Racso looked around.

The noise came again. It was harsh and scraping.

"It's coming from the creek, somewhere beyond the bend," Isabella said. Her voice had become a whisper, and she looked scared.

"We'd better hide!" Racso motioned toward the underbrush at the top of the bank. Isabella started to worm her way into the thicket, but the basket on her back became tangled in the branches. She struggled desperately. "Calm down!" Racso whispered. He helped her slip the harness off her shoulders. The basket came free and rolled down the slope toward the water. Isabella started to go after it, but

Racso grabbed her by the paw and pulled her into the thicket.

"I heard voices," he whispered. "And they didn't sound like us."

"What *did* they sound like?" Isabella's eyes were huge.

"Like . . ." Racso hesitated. Could it be true? "Like humans," he whispered.

Something flashed in the winter sunlight. Where Timothy stood, partway up the mountain, he could see it clearly in the center of the wiggly green creek. It was about a mile to the west of Emerald Pond, and it was glittering. Brendan saw it, too.

"I think it's a boat," he said.

Timothy couldn't take his eyes from the silvery spot. On the mountain he was a spectator, but those who were close to the creek—even the rats at home in the nest—were in danger. He remembered Racso's assignment. He and Isabella were mapping the creek just east of Emerald Pond.

"We've got to warn everyone," he said. "And if it is a boat—and if it has people in it—we've got to make sure they don't make it all the way to the pond!"

Timothy closed his eyes. Could it be a bad dream? But when he opened them again, the silver spot was still there, moving slowly. He even thought he could see two tiny black dots inside it. People.

"We've got to tell Justin," Brendan said.

Timothy reached into his knapsack and took out a reed whistle. He blew it hard. A long, shrill call floated down the mountain. In the valley gray heads turned and looked up. Feet began running toward the sound.

Racso and Isabella heard the whistle, but they were too scared to move. The boat had come around the bend, and suddenly it was right in front of them. When it bumped a rock in the water they heard the scraping sound again.

"There's a little beach," a voice said. "Let's eat lunch."

Isabella wouldn't open her eyes. She seemed to be frozen stiff. Racso tried to calm her. "The boat is called a canoe, and the two wooden sticks are paddles," he whispered in her ear. "The American Indians used canoes. I know because I saw one in the movie *The Last of the Mohicans*. . . . There's a man and a woman in the boat. She has long red hair and glasses, and the man has a black beard and a knitted cap a little bit like mine. They're right alongside the shore now. . . . They're getting out. . . . They're pulling the canoe up on the sand. . . . They're going to sit on that old elm log just beneath us!"

Isabella shuddered. Racso held her paw comfortingly. He couldn't talk anymore, because the people were so close.

The man's voice was deep and strong. "How did you end up covering the dam story, Lindsey?"

"I was one of the reporters at the state legislature when the money for the dam was passed," the young woman answered. "Representative Jones sponsored the bill. At the time I thought it was strange that he would do that, since most of his district is farmland. Sure enough, when I went to some of the public meetings held by the farmers, they opposed the dam, on the ground that it would destroy their livelihood. But other people argued that this land is just being wasted as it is now."

"Wasted!" The man shook his head sorrowfully. "There are only a few wilderness areas left in this state, and Thorn Valley's the largest. If it's destroyed, all the animals that live here will die, too."

"That's one of the reasons I asked you to come with me, Jack. If you take some photographs, I'll try to get them printed in the paper. That way, people will have a chance to see what Thorn Valley is like."

"I'm surprised other people haven't come here to go hiking or canoeing."

Lindsey took a bite of her sandwich. "Before the construction company blasted a road through the mountain, the valley was almost inaccessible," she said. "The north end is a deep gorge, and where it ends the river goes over a series of falls too steep for boating."

Jack stood up and stretched. "I'll set up my tripod right here. We'll get some shots of the creek and that old walnut tree behind it. And then we'll do some of the mountain over there to the west."

"Great! But we can't take too long. I want you to get some pictures of the gorge, too, and the area where the dam construction is going on."

Christopher and Sally were on the west side of the creek when the whistle blew. They had not seen or heard the boat and were only half finished with their map. Christopher was climbing a tall pine tree. He had figured that the view from its top limbs would show every curve along the west bank of the creekbed. That would make finishing the map an easy job. When he heard the whistle he couldn't believe his ears. Who could be in trouble? And where? The noise sounded as if it had come from the mountain. They were supposed to run immediately in the direction of the sound, but Christopher had a better idea. He decided to crawl out on a branch to see what the problem was.

When she finished her sandwich, Lindsey rinsed her hands off in the creek.

"Brrr," she said. "The water's freezing." She bent over. "What's this?"

Jack went and stood beside her. "I'll be darned! There must have been people here, and not too long ago!" His back was to Racso. He seemed to be poking at something with his finger.

"It looks like a toy, but it's beautifully made."

"It couldn't have been here long, or it would have rotted."

"Look at these vines. . . . They're almost like a little harness!"

The woman turned back, toward the bank. Now—his eyes wide with horror—Racso could see the basket cradled in her hand.

*   *   *

The moment he spent on the limb of the pine tree seemed to Christopher like the longest moment of his whole life. He had never seen humans before, had never expected to see them, so that he felt as if he were in a dream. When the one with red hair picked up the basket—one of their baskets, he felt sure, though how it could have gotten there was more than he could guess—he had to do something. But what?

Below him he could hear Sally.

"Christopher! Come down out of that tree! We're supposed to go as soon as the whistle blows. Christopher! Didn't you hear the whistle? We're going to get in big trouble. Come back down here!"

He had to shut her up! He leaned over and waved the bottom part of the branch desperately, trying to signal that there was trouble. He was afraid to call out loud.

Bending over on the tip of the limb, he heard the branch begin to crack. Later, that was all he remembered.

The red-haired woman whirled around when she heard the crash. She grabbed Jack by the arm.

"What was that?"

"It came from the pine tree across the creek, I think. See—the branches are still moving. We may have scared an animal that was nesting there."

"It gave me the creeps. I feel like someone was spying on us."

"Want to have a look?"

She laughed nervously. "I think I'll stay here. You go."

Racso watched carefully as the man launched the canoe and ferried carefully across the creek. He got out on the opposite shore, climbed up the bank, and pushed through thick underbrush to get to the tree. Racso himself did not know what had made the crashing sound; he expected that it was simply the falling of an old branch. What he did know was what had happened to the basket. The woman had dropped it when she whirled around.

It was in plain view on the ground, about a foot in front of the elm log where the people had sat to eat lunch. The woman was facing the opposite shore, her hands stuck into the pockets of her green parka. Racso was not sure he could get it, but he felt he had to try. If they took it with them, they might figure out that it was not a toy. And then what?

He whispered to Isabella to stay put, then crept

to the edge of the thicket. The woman hadn't moved. Racso came out of the bramble and braced himself carefully as he descended the bank, step by step.

"Jack? Did you find anything?"

Silence.

"Jack? JACK?"

"Lindsey, I'll be back over there in a minute. . . ." Jack's voice came from the underbrush.

Racso reached the elm log and crouched behind it. His lungs felt as if they were ready to burst, and he realized that he'd been holding his breath. He breathed slowly, steadily—they'd practiced that in the training sessions. He could see the woman's hiking boots, still turned toward the creek. Slowly he crept over the log, down onto the sand. His steps were slow, silent, but his heart was pounding.

The basket was just an inch from his nose when he heard the paddle clank against the side of the aluminum canoe. The man was coming back! Racso grabbed the basket in his mouth and ran up the bank, dodging through frozen stalks of milkweed. When he got to the top he looked back. The woman was helping Jack pull the canoe back onto the sand. They hadn't seen him at all.

"There was blood," Jack said. "It was still warm. And the branch was there, too, a fairly small one.

It was rotted most of the way through. It must have collapsed under the weight of the animal."

"So someone *was* spying on us," she said.

"I don't blame them, whoever they are. This is their valley. They have reason to fear us."

"They can't know that."

"They can sense it."

"What do you think it was?"

"A raccoon or possum, probably. Too bad I didn't get a shot of it when I took the photographs."

She seemed reassured at the thought of a raccoon. "We'd better get back on the river," she said. "It's quarter of one."

He nodded. "What did you do with that little basket?"

"I must have dropped it when I heard the crash."

They both bent over the sand, looking. She walked back toward the elm log and rummaged through the milkweed stalks. She even looked up the bank toward the thicket. But it was nowhere to be found.

"You must have dropped it into the creek," Jack said. "The water swept it away."

"Maybe . . ." She frowned. "It sure was strange. Who would have brought a little kid, with toys, into the wilderness?"

Jack grinned. He pulled the canoe around so that

it was facing downstream. "Maybe it belonged to your spy," he said, swinging his leg over the side of the boat.

"Very funny!" She rolled her eyes, grabbed the remaining paddle from the beach, and clambered into the front of the canoe. Their paddles dipped into the dark green water once, twice, three times, and the canoe went out of sight around the bend.

The Nightmare

Christopher lay in bed in the infirmary. His eyes were closed and his breathing was slow and labored. Elvira thought that he had a punctured lung. He would be in bed for the whole month of February. She was worried. She let Timothy and Racso look in on Christopher from the doorway for five minutes before she shooed them away.

"Is he going to be all right?" Racso hated to ask the question, but he couldn't help himself.

Elvira didn't look directly at him when she answered. "I don't know. It's a dangerous time of year to be sick. The cold makes it harder to recover."

"I don't want him to die!"

"Of course you don't! None of us does!" Elvira snapped.

"I had pneumonia, and I got over it," Timothy said softly.

Elvira smiled, but her tone was brusque. "You were lucky."

"He's going to be fine," Racso said stubbornly. "You'll see."

Justin was proud of Racso for recovering the wicker basket, and of Sally for dragging Christopher to safety after he had fallen from the pine tree. The training had been fruitful. The rats had found themselves in a crisis and had responded well. But the fact that humans had come into the valley was a very bad sign. Though they had seemed sympathetic to the wilderness, there was no reason to believe that— should they have stumbled upon the colony—they would have kept quiet about it. After all, journalists wanted news. So Justin assigned a sentry to keep watch over the valley from the mountainside. He ordered the gardens and the playground dismantled, and the entrance holes to the nest covered with branches. And he pushed the rats in the training program to do more, so that they would be prepared for any emergency.

In the mornings before school the rats ran a mile without stopping. Sometimes they ran in a group, but other times they were assigned to run in pairs or by themselves. They were given a course to complete by a certain time, and they knew that someone would be waiting to see whether they got there when they were supposed to. In the evenings they studied a textbook ordered from a computer company, memorizing the symbols that make up the special language of computers. They made mock computer keyboards and practiced composing and entering simple programs on them. Justin kept time, pushing them to work faster, congratulating the rats who met deadlines and consoling those who didn't.

Sometimes, after the hardest sessions, Racso cried. He did not tell the others, not even Timothy; but there were times when he simply felt he could not do what was required of him. He tried as hard as he could, and failed. Other rats failed, too; but they didn't seem to take it as hard as Racso. They tried to cheer him up: "There's always tomorrow, you know." But Racso would walk away with his teeth clenched and his hat jammed down over his ears.

He would find a private spot in the raspberry bushes, and there the tears would fall. As he cried he would find that the disappointment eased a little, and he felt more relaxed. Sometimes by the time he left he felt positively cheerful.

Isabella was having a tantrum. The other rats watched quietly as she jumped up and down. Her tail flailed back and forth.

"You can't do this to me!" she screamed. "You just can't!"

Justin tried for the third time to finish a sentence. "I'm sorry if your feelings—"

"NO! NO! NO!" Isabella hurled herself on the ground. "I love you! I won't leave!"

Justin tried again. "We talked, and we don't feel that you—"

"NOOOOOOO!" Isabella shouted. And then she began to weep.

"It was because she panicked when she saw the humans," Brendan whispered conspiratorially. "They figured she couldn't stand up to the pressure of the mission if she couldn't get through that."

"Anyone can panic," Sally said. "I don't think she

should be thrown out of the training program just because she panicked."

"In an emergency you have to be able to control your emotions," Beatrice said. "Otherwise you won't be able to do what you're supposed to."

"Look at Racso," Brendan said. "He sat there, he realized what had to be done, and he did it."

"But he must have been afraid," Sally argued. "Anyone is afraid in a dangerous situation. It makes sense to be afraid."

"Fear and panic are different." Beatrice looked as if she were about to say more but she turned to Racso instead. "How *did* you feel?"

He hesitated. "I *was* scared, I think—at least I remember that my heart was pounding. But I wasn't as scared as Isabella, because I'm used to humans. I've been around them a lot. I knew they wouldn't be able to catch me if they started chasing me. And I figured if they saw me they'd probably think I was a muskrat."

"So you were able to figure things out even though you were scared," Brendan said. "That was good!"

Racso smiled. Brendan had given him a compliment! His chest swelled. In fact, everyone seemed to be smiling at him. They liked him!

He was as surprised by what happened next as the others. His mouth opened, and he heard himself say, "I told a lie."

"What?" The other rats looked surprised.

"Do you mean that you didn't tell the truth about how you felt when you saw the people?" Beatrice asked.

"Not that. . . ." Racso felt the blood running to his head. But he had started to tell them, and he might as well finish. "About my family . . . about living in a mansion with rich people. That wasn't true. I just wanted to impress you, so I made it up. There's more, too." A lump formed in his throat. "But I can't tell you everything now. I'm just not ready."

"You lied about your background." It was Brendan again, and this time he sounded tough. "Why should we believe anything you say?"

"Because I admitted it," Racso said. "Nobody forced me to tell you. I wanted you to know."

Beatrice nodded. "That's true . . . nobody forced him."

"I'm glad you told us," Sally said. "I never really believed all that stuff, anyway."

"But when will you tell us the truth?" Brendan's tone was sharp.

"I don't know . . ." Racso faltered.

Suddenly Sally grinned. "Stay tuned for the next dramatic chapter of Racso the rat's 'True Confessions' . . . coming we don't know when on another channel. . . ." Everyone laughed, even Racso.

"Is that really what TV sounds like?" Brendan asked seriously.

Racso nodded. "You just have to make your voice a little deeper. Like this . . ."

Christopher was worse. He had gotten a virus, and he wouldn't eat. He was so sick that he hardly opened his eyes. Elvira told his parents, and they told Nicodemus. Nicodemus told Justin and Hermione. Hermione told the rats in the schoolroom. She tried to be upbeat, but after she spoke, the room was as silent as a tomb. Then Sally began to cry.

"It's my fault. If I hadn't started yelling for him to come down he would never have fallen. He was trying to signal me to be quiet."

"You saved him." Hermione's voice was firm. "If the humans had found Christopher, they probably would have taken him with them in their boat and tried to care for him. A veterinarian would have told them he was a Norway rat. They might have begun to ask questions: Why were domestic rats nesting in the middle of a wilderness? When Christopher woke up he might have cried out, not realizing where he was. And then what? It wouldn't have taken them long to connect the talking rat with the little basket. They would have been back." Hermione hesitated. "And they would have known what they were looking for."

Sally's heart had stopped, and her mouth was open in an "O." She had not really thought about what *could* have happened.

"It was scary to hear a big animal coming up the bank when I was trying to help Christopher. I dragged him behind an oak tree and covered him up with leaves, and then I ran back and wiped up the blood. I missed some of it, though, because that was the first thing the man saw."

"How did you feel when you saw the man?"

"Terrified." Sally laughed. "I dug myself under the leaves right beside Christopher and didn't look out again until he was gone."

"You were lucky he wasn't an Indian scout," Racso said. "They know how to track animals. If he'd been an Indian he would have found you."

"Indian scouts don't paddle metal canoes," Brendan pointed out.

"I know, but—"

"STOP!"

The whole class turned in astonishment. Timothy was on his feet. His body was taut.

"Someone may be dying, and we're sitting here laughing and talking nonsense!"

Hermione's voice was gentle. "We're doing everything we can for Christopher."

"Not everything!" Timothy was adamant. "Mr. Ages gave me a special powder three years ago when I had pneumonia. I asked Elvira about it, but she says the plant it's made from doesn't grow in the valley."

"The trip to Mr. Fitzgibbon's farm in midwinter could take weeks, Timothy. It would be dangerous. And more lives would be risked."

"We'll be risking lives at the damsite."

"To save many lives—all the animals who live here."

"I still think we can do more for Christopher."

When Timothy sat down, the whole class stared at him. No one had ever heard him argue or raise his voice. Could he be the same mouse who had occupied that seat for the past three years? He looked the same: bright eyes, soft gray fur, long whiskers. But something had changed.

*   *   *

"I just mean that I've never seen you like that before!"

Racso and Timothy were in their room, sitting on Timothy's bed. "You've always been so . . . good. What's wrong with you?"

"Nothing's wrong with me! Do you think you're the only one who can argue?"

"Nooo . . ." Racso was mystified. "It's just that I'm not used to you doing it, I guess."

Timothy was silent for a moment. Looking at him, Racso noticed that his eyes looked glazed, as if he also were sick.

"Are you sure you're all right, Timothy?" he asked plaintively. "You just don't look like yourself."

Timothy stared at the floor.

"Timothy?" Racso touched his shoulder with one paw.

"No," Timothy said. And he looked away. "Three nights ago I had a dream. I'm not sure whether it was about me or Christopher—during the dream we seemed to be the same. But it was awful."

"What happened?"

Timothy put his face between his paws. "I dreamed that I was in Christopher's bed in the infirmary and that I was going to die. And I could see into the future, because for me there would be no future. My bed lifted up and flew out the window, like a magic carpet. I leaned over the side and could see things changing—slowly, at first, but then faster and faster."

Racso was spellbound. "What kind of things?"

"I saw the dam being built. The valley began to fill up with water. I saw the rats leaving, going single file over the mountain, carrying their tools on their backs. Many of the other animals stayed too long, and drowned. Their screams were horrible."

Timothy paused. His voice was weak.

"Finally the valley became a great lake, and there were more than twenty roads coming to it. Each road was crowded with cars, and every car was filled with people. Some parts of the valley that had remained above water were turned into parking lots. There were metal garbage cans, and the animals that were left crept out at night to eat from them, because there was no place else to get food.

"I flew on in my bed, following one of the highways, and I saw the Fitzgibbons' house, with a road running beside it where the bean field used to be. When I came closer, I saw a sign out front that said 'Antiques.' There was no garden, and the water in the brook looked dark and oily. Where the barn had stood I saw a restaurant with a big plastic statue of a monkey holding a plate of sandwiches.

"I signaled the bed to come down, and it landed in the Fitzgibbons' old garden. The big stone was still there, but for a minute I didn't see our cinder-block house. Then when I did see it, I was afraid to go inside. The entrance was blocked with bits of paper and broken glass. I pushed my way through. I called out, but no one answered. The living room was awful! It was littered with bits of junk. In one corner there was a little pile of dried grass.

"The bedroom was empty. I left and walked toward the brook. I found my family there: my mother, Cynthia and Teresa. Mother hugged me tight.

" 'Martin's taken Breta and the children and gone away,' she said. 'He said he couldn't stand it here any longer.' I saw her brush away tears. 'We've had to change the way we live, Timothy.'

"They were gaunt, and their fur looked coarse and patchy.

" 'We've decided to live by the brook all year round now,' Mother said. 'The sound of the water is soothing. We couldn't get used to the noise from the highway.'

" 'What do you eat?'

" 'We've learned to live on the scraps that people throw away. Mostly meat and bits of fried potato.'

" 'What about water?'

" 'We drink from the brook,' Teresa said. 'It's oily, but you get used to it after a while.'

"Cynthia pushed her way through the others.

" 'Are you going to stay, Timothy? Are you going to stay here with us? We've missed you so much—'

" 'He can't stay, Cynthia,' my mother interrupted. 'One of his friends is very sick. Without Timothy, Christopher may die.'

" 'But how can *I* help him?' My voice rose in desperation.

" 'Don't give up. . . .' Her voice seemed to fade.

" 'How? Tell me *how*!' I said.

"And then I woke up."

Timothy sat quietly on the bed. He felt exhausted. Racso sat beside him, pondering the dream.

"You must tell Nicodemus," he said suddenly.

Timothy looked surprised. He nodded slowly.

"Go tomorrow morning," Racso said. "He'll know what to do."

To Save a Friend

Nicodemus looked tired and old.

"I understand how you feel, after that awful dream," he said. "But I just don't see how we can do it."

Justin nodded. "It would be a terrible trip. And the sky looks like snow."

"Let me try," Timothy begged. "If only I could get the medicine from Mr. Ages . . ."

"No." Nicodemus was adamant.

"Isn't there anyone else who could go? It could mean Christopher's life." Timothy was getting desperate.

Nicodemus regarded him levelly. "We can't give

up one life to save another—and that's what we would be doing. The mountain is covered with ice. The descent on the other side would be impossible."

"There must be some way. . . ." Timothy's eyes lit up suddenly. "What about Jeremy?"

Justin shook his head sadly. "He's not due in for another week. And we have no way to contact him."

"We have the emergency signal for the couriers. Another crow could drop the message at Jeremy's nest!"

Justin looked thoughtful. "I think it's worth a try," he told Nicodemus. "I could go up this afternoon and set up the signal."

Nicodemus nodded. "Do it, then. But you"—he turned to Timothy—"don't get your hopes up. There's a storm brewing. We may not have a courier until it's over—and that could mean days."

"All right." But Timothy felt a rising excitement. If they could get the medicine, surely Christopher would get better!

"He's too sick to eat," Racso told Isabella. She was in the kitchen, her paws deep in a vat of acorn flour.

"It's terrible." Isabella shook her head. "I wish there was something I could do for him. Believe me,

I know what it is to suffer. This last week has been the worst of my whole life."

"That's different. You don't have something physically wrong with you."

"Rats die from broken hearts, too, you know." Isabella paused. "I never thought Justin would treat me this way. After all my years of devotion . . ."

"I think you're taking it too personally. Other rats have been asked to leave the training program, too."

Isabella stuck out her upper lip in a pout. "The others would have reacted the same way I did, if they'd seen people. Justin just expected too much of me. He has higher standards for me, because I'm special."

That made Racso mad. "All you can think about is yourself! Everyone else is just as special as you are. Look at me! I made the long trip from the city all by myself. And I know about a lot of things you don't: telephones and rock stars and movies and Indians and video games and candy—"

"SHUT UP, Racso! You're nothing but an obnoxious little runt!"

"I won't shut up!" Racso was so mad he felt like biting Isabella. Calling him a runt! He bared his teeth and growled.

"BITE ME!" Isabella flung her paws out wide to

each side, to show that she wouldn't try to defend herself. "Go ahead and bite me, Racso! BITE ME!"

Racso felt stupid. "I'm not going to bite you, Isabella."

"Aha! You're afraid I'd tell Justin, aren't you?"

"I'm not afraid of anything!" But secretly Racso was afraid. Biting was against the rules at Thorn Valley. And Isabella was doing the best she could to make him break the rules.

"Aren't you just little Mister Know-it-all!" she shouted. "Movie stars, potato chips, go-carts, candy! Maybe we ought to bow down and worship you, you know so much!"

"Shut up, Isabella." But Racso's anger had left him. His mind repeated her phrase, ending with the word "candy." Candy! He and Christopher had planned to make candy, and now Christopher was dying. He might never get to taste candy. If only he could eat one piece! Christopher loved new things— he had worn the headband every day, had jabbered away in backward language, had sung "Sweet Lorinda" until he'd almost driven the others crazy.

"Isabella!" Racso forgot the argument. His voice was hushed with excitement. "We might be able to help Christopher, you and I."

"*What?*"

"We might be able to save him. Sit down!"

Isabella sat. She listened, trying to be patient, while Racso unfolded a plan.

The mountain path was icy, but the sentries had cut steps into the ice and had strung ropes along the steepest sections to keep themselves from falling. Justin and Beatrice climbed slowly, without speaking. The wind whipped through their fur. A coating of ice formed on their whiskers. The sky was gray and overcast.

After an hour they reached the sentry's post, where a small fire was burning. A rat stood beside it, warming his paws.

"Justin! I didn't expect to see you up here! Shift change isn't for another three hours! And Beatrice, too!"

"We've come to try to signal a courier," Justin explained, warming himself at the fire. "Christopher is much worse. We're going to try to send a message to Mr. Ages."

"For medicine?"

Beatrice nodded. "He has a white powder made from the roots of a plant that doesn't grow in the valley. Timothy had it when he was sick three years ago, and it helped him. He's the one who insisted we try to get it."

"I don't think anyone's going to be flying on a day like this," the sentry muttered. "There's a winter storm blowing in."

"We can try." Justin fetched the gleaming white stones that were kept piled beside the wall of the cliff and set them in a pyramid on the flat rock near the sentry's post. "After all, it could mean Christopher's life."

"He's that bad off?"

Justin nodded. "He's unconscious, and Elvira hasn't been able to get him to eat or drink. He's strong, but she doesn't know how long he can last if he doesn't take a turn for the better."

"Poor kid." The sentry sighed.

Beatrice produced a letter from her knapsack. "If anyone responds to the signal, we need this taken to the old foundation just beyond the Fitzgibbons' farm. It should be dropped in an obvious place. Explain that there's an old white mouse living there, that he's a doctor, and that no harm must come to him. His powders have saved many lives, including birds'."

"All right."

"There's another message, too, for Jeremy. It should be dropped at his nest. We're asking him to fly the powder here if it's safe to do so."

"Got it." The sentry nodded smartly. "Sure you don't want to warm up a little more before you head back?"

"We'll be fine," Beatrice said. They nodded good-bye.

Timothy walked with Racso past the bare garden plots, toward the pond. He felt better. It felt good to have told the nightmare to Racso and then Nicodemus. It was almost as if he had been able to hand over the responsibility for Christopher to someone else. Not that he didn't want to be responsible—he *did*. It was just that the dream had made him feel so bad that he couldn't think about what to do. All he could do was feel upset.

"Dreams aren't real," Nicodemus had said. "But often they represent fears that are real. It's not surprising that in the dream your worry about Christopher changed itself into worry about your family and Thorn Valley. You care a great deal about both of them."

"That makes sense," Racso said, when Timothy

told him. "After all, they're both in danger."

Timothy swatted at the frozen dirt near the edge of the pond. "I'd run away before I'd live at the place I saw in that dream," he said. "I couldn't stand that."

"You should stop worrying about it. Arthur and Justin have finished the plan for the sabotage mission. They're going to unveil it at the training session tomorrow night."

"If only the plan succeeds . . ."

"Timothy, look!" Racso pointed toward the western sky. "Look, isn't that a bird up by the cliff?"

Timothy squinted at a dark object only a little bigger than a dot. "I think you're right! And it looks like it's going to land!"

"If only it agrees to take the message to Mr. Ages!"

"If only . . ." Timothy nodded, then smiled wryly. "That seems to sum it up right now, doesn't it?"

"Timothy!" Racso's mouth opened, and then it twitched at the corners, as if he wasn't sure whether to smile or frown. "Look! It's snowing!"

The infirmary was dark and quiet. Elvira sat in the corner by the window on a chair made from a curved tree root. She rocked herself back and forth gently. Near her, on a low mattress stuffed with feathers, lay Christopher. His eyes were closed. His chest rose and fell slightly with each breath. Except for that, he was perfectly still.

Occasionally Elvira glanced out the window. Snow blew past in a steady stream. Once she got up and fetched a vial of something from the burner stove in the laboratory. She stirred it and poured it into a small wooden bowl. With a spoon she poured a bit of the liquid into the sleeping rat's mouth, but immediately he choked, so that the broth ran out his mouth and down the gray fur of his cheek. Elvira sighed deeply.

"Christopher, I want you to drink," she said.

But there was no sign that Christopher heard anything at all.

The snow continued to drift past the window. How much time passed, how many hours, before the gentle rap came on the door? Elvira, dozing in her chair, was not sure. She rose and opened it. A pair of rats stood side by side.

"Come in."

The female hesitated. "Is he . . ."

"Better? No." Elvira's voice was gentle. "But not really worse. He's stronger than he looks."

"He hasn't eaten in almost a week." The male rat sounded hoarse, as if he found it difficult to speak.

"How much longer can he go on like this?"

"I'm not sure." Elvira shook her head, as if she, too, were puzzled and upset. "Another day or two, perhaps."

"There's nothing more you can do?"

"Not right now."

Christopher's mother stifled a sob. "He's our only child."

"It's possible that he could recover," Elvira said softly. "Try not to despair. Talk to him. He may hear you, even though he can't respond."

So the two rats sat down beside the bed and spoke in low voices as the snow continued to fall.

When Isabella and Racso met in the kitchen, it was past midnight. Isabella started a fire in the stove. Then she showed Racso how to grind the dried mint into a smooth paste.

"Add beet sugar. Now more water. It has to be smoother than that, Racso!" Isabella was in command. She took the grinding stone away and showed Racso how to scrape it against the bottom of the bowl, using first one paw, then the other. Racso tried again. After just a few minutes his front legs started to ache. He could hear himself grunting out loud with each push.

With a shake of her head Isabella took the bowl away. She tested the mixture with a spoon, then added soybean milk and a bit of acorn flour. She showed Racso how to form the mixture into small, flat cakes. While he did that Isabella mixed carob, sugar, and peanut oil in a pan on the stove. She took the little cakes one by one and dipped them in the hot carob, then set them on a wooden slab to harden.

"The cookbook says they should cool for at least an hour. So we'll have to wait."

"But I want to taste it," Racso wheedled. "Just one. Please, Isabella."

"Absolutely not." Isabella marched back and forth in front of the candy as if she were guarding a cache of jewels. Racso sat forlornly in the middle of the kitchen. The candy smelled lovely. Minutes seemed like hours.

"If it works," Racso reminded himself, "if the candy saves Christopher's life, this will be a great achievement."

Isabella grunted. "And don't forget that it couldn't have been accomplished without me. *I* found the recipe and started the fire in the stove and showed you how to grind the paste. And *I* made the carob coating."

Racso nodded. He had to admit that Isabella deserved some of the credit.

"Wait until Justin hears about this," Isabella said.

"An hour's up!" Racso charged the platter, grabbed the closest candy, and crammed it into his mouth whole. Its gooey sweetness seemed to fill his whole body like a wonderful dream. "More!" he shouted. "I need more!"

"You most certainly do not," Isabella said. "The rest is for Christopher."

Two hours before dawn the sentries came down from the mountain. The snow had become so thick that it was impossible to keep the fire lighted, and without the fire they could not stay on the cliff face. By the time they reached the nest, their fur was coated with ice, and their paws and legs were numb. They woke Justin and told him of their decision to abandon the post. He winced sympathetically as he watched them limp toward the infirmary.

"A bad night to be out," Elvira said crisply. She rubbed their paws with snow until the feeling began to return. Justin stood watching.

"You'll never guess who picked up that letter you and Beatrice brought up," one of the sentries remarked.

"Who?"

"A horned owl." The rat shook his head, as if even the memory of the owl was intimidating. "A really big one. To tell you the truth, I thought he was coming after me—I was terrified! But after he landed he just nodded toward the pile of stones. I gave him the papers with the instructions you'd told me and he nodded again. And then he took off."

Justin was surprised and pleased.

"How's the kid doing?"

"Better than you'd be now if you hadn't left the mountain the moment you did," Elvira said darkly. "You took a real chance, you know. Another fifteen minutes and I don't think you'd have made it down."

"Ooooooow! It hurts."

"That means you can feel." Elvira stopped rubbing for a moment. "We can be thankful for that. By tomorrow, you should be as good as new."

Racso wrapped two pieces of candy in birch-bark paper and hid the paper inside his hat. Then he put the hat on his head. He spent a half hour trying to think of ways to sneak past Elvira so that he could be alone with Christopher. But when he got to the infirmary just after dawn, Elvira was asleep in her chair. Racso tiptoed in. He stood beside his friend, watching his chest move up and down.

"Christopher." He spoke in a whisper. "I brought you something to eat."

Christopher didn't answer. His eyes stayed closed. His chest rose and fell slowly.

"It's what we picked the mint for," Racso whispered. "Remember the stuff I told you about, that I used to eat back in the city? We made some for you. Some candy."

Racso wished Christopher would open his eyes or move at all, even one paw, but he didn't.

"I'll just put a bit of it in your mouth, so you can see how good it tastes," Racso said. He broke off a corner from one piece of candy. He opened Christopher's mouth gently and put the candy on top of his tongue. "You can just let it melt if you don't feel like chewing right now. It's good that way, too."

Christopher was still. Racso thought for a moment that he was dead. He was relieved when he saw Christopher breathe one more time. At the same time he felt scared and disappointed. Maybe the candy wouldn't help. Maybe Christopher was going to die after all. Maybe he would never see his friend alive again.

"Christopher," he whispered, "I have to leave."

Christopher was still.

"I'll sing your favorite song," Racso said. He felt so much like crying that he could hardly sing, but he made himself do it anyway. The song was made to be sung really loud, but Racso did the best he could, singing softly:

> Sweet Lorinda,
> Lorinda, my love,
> Your touch reminds me
> Of a soft turtle dove.
>
> Your eyes are lovely,
> Like the stars at night.
> Stay with me, darling,
> Tonight, tonight.

The Master Plan

Outside, the snow lay drifted in deep piles. The sky was clear, a dark blue, with a pale slice of moon hovering just above the horizon. From outside the closed windows of the cafeteria, you could hear the muffled clatter of wooden bowls. Looking in, you could see the glow of candles forming soft yellow circles in the shadowed rooms and hallways.

The meeting room was empty. Over the winter it had been transformed. Diagrams of the dam covered the walls. A time frame listed the steps involved in building the dam and the date by which each step should be finished. There were drawings of all the sections of the damsite and the operations center, a cinder-block building on the east side of the river. The computer was housed there. Below, in the basement, the pictures showed a set of emergency generators, to be used in the event of a power failure. An electric cable ran through a narrow tunnel in the mountainside and supplied the energy to operate the computer and the dam.

Timothy had studied the drawings so many times that he knew them by heart. Even so, he paused in front of them before he sat down. Racso, Sally, and Brendan followed suit. The other members of the training unit came in one by one. There was no joking, no teasing, no easy banter. When Arthur and Justin appeared in the doorway, the room was completely quiet.

Justin spoke slowly. "Today I'll present what you've been waiting for: the master plan for the sabotage of the computer and the dam. The plan will not be easy to accomplish; it will take skill and intelligence and stamina. But we think it can be done."

Justin paused. The room was so tense that the air felt electric. He outlined the plan:

"We will leave here in two weeks and establish a headquarters and living quarters adjacent to the damsite. We'll set up a security force and do all our work under their supervision, at night. During the first two weeks we'll become familiar with the layout of the site and with the computer. We'll study the computer manual and make copies of the programs that are in use.

"The next month will be spent practicing with the computer. Each night we'll enter parts of our program, check them, then erase them before we have to leave. We'll open the computer and study the circuitry inside it. We'll study the gates and spillways of the dam itself, and the mechanisms that open and close them.

"Security will be crucial. The humans will be checking their equipment carefully. They must never notice that it has been tampered with. If they did, they might increase the number of watchmen guarding the site at night. That could make our work impossible.

"Our program will be entered into the computer once and for all on the night before the grand opening ceremony. There are risks to this—many risks. We will have only one night to accomplish all that must be done. But the grand opening will have an audience of thousands. If it is a disaster—and we plan to make it a disaster—the people will be angry.

They will think the Joneses are incompetent. And they will not want more money spent on the dam."

"But if the computer has a different program in it, they'll figure out that someone else was involved," Brendan observed.

Justin held up one paw. "Let me finish. Our plan is that the computer and the program inside it will be destroyed. But as an extra precaution, Arthur has worked things out so that our program closely resembles the real program. Under close inspection it will appear that someone accidentally typed the wrong information into the computer."

Arthur stepped forward. He had printed two columns of figures on the blackboard behind him.

"These numbers represent the formula the humans used to figure out the speed at which the dam's gates will open and close. They used information like the pressure exerted by tons of water on the face of the dam and the thickness and weight of the gates themselves to arrive at what they think is a safe speed." Arthur smiled. "We've used their formula to calculate the opposite: the unsafe speed." He pointed to the second row of figures. "These are the numbers we'll be typing into the program. They will cause the gates to rise so fast that their intense vibrations will shatter the concrete wall of the dam."

Sally looked confused. "You mean we'll be typing numbers into their program?"

Arthur shook his head. "It would be easier if we could. But their program is designed with certain limits that ensure the safety of the dam. As it is now, their program would shut off if we inserted the numbers that we want to. Our program will have no safety limits."

Racso raised his paw. "How are we going to wreck the computer?"

"I was getting to that." Arthur smiled again. "We'll be placing a fuse between two electrical connections inside the machine. We'll soak the fuse in oil first, to make it more flammable. The next time the program is activated, the fuse will ignite. The fire will creep along a piece of twine to a small heap of blasting powder—for that, we'll figure about an hour from the time the program begins. The explosion will be strong enough to destroy the inside of the computer without hurting anyone standing nearby."

"It sounds good." Beatrice seemed to be thinking out loud. "But you've left out one part that we all want to hear."

Arthur and Justin both looked startled. "What do you mean?"

"You haven't said who is going."

There was a slight stir in the room. It was hard not to look around and think about who had performed better or worse during the training sessions; who might be needed more at home; who was strong enough and brave enough and smart enough to be chosen to go on the mission.

Justin looked as if he wanted to say more, but all he said was "The names will be posted on the door of this room next Monday."

Just before the session ended, Hermione came in. She was smiling.

"I've got good news! Christopher regained consciousness for a moment this afternoon. He's still very sick, but it's a good sign."

"Hurray!" The atmosphere in the room seemed suddenly changed, from dreadful seriousness to a warm, nice feeling. Timothy felt a smile spread from ear to ear, and when he looked toward Racso, the smile was mirrored on his friend's face. Even Justin was smiling, as if for that moment the plan didn't even matter.

"He spoke," Hermione said. "Elvira wasn't sure what he meant, but she heard the word clearly. He said 'More.' "

Racso was nervous about telling Elvira about the candy, but it turned out there was no need for him to tell her because Isabella already had. She told the whole story in Elvira's office, next to the infirmary. Christopher's parents were there, and near the end, Racso, Timothy, and Justin came in, too.

"I've been tired all day, but the sacrifice was worth it," she proclaimed. "I was up till four o'clock this morning, you know. Making candy is a lot of work."

Elvira sounded puzzled. "But I never saw you come in. And I was with Christopher all night, except for when the sentries came in—and that was earlier."

Isabella looked embarrassed. "Actually, it was my helper who gave the candy to Christopher."

"Your helper?"

She nodded. Racso was standing in the doorway, and Isabella pointed toward him. "Racso."

"Racso!" Elvira looked more and more astounded. "But Racso never came in, either!"

Racso was unsure about what to say, but Isabella didn't give him much time to say anything. "He sneaked in and put some candy in Christopher's mouth, and it just dissolved there. And when Christopher tasted it, he knew he had to wake up to get another piece."

Elvira looked at Racso. "Is this true?"

He nodded. "You were asleep in your chair."

"Were you afraid to ask?"

"He was just so sick . . . I thought you might think it would make him worse."

Elvira smiled. Racso had never seen her smile like that. She looked gentle and kind, like someone's fairy godmother. She asked, "Where's the rest of the candy?"

"It's hidden in the storeroom, in the basket where we kept the mint."

"Go get it," Elvira said. "We may never know exactly what helped Christopher, but he does seem better. And if it was the candy, then we should give him some more."

Racso ran down the hall to the storeroom and took three pieces of candy out of the basket. It was only on the way back that he started to think harder about what was happening. Isabella had lied! She had claimed credit for the candy. As if it had been her idea in the first place! As if she had picked the mint and hidden it all winter in the storeroom! As if she had been the one who had realized that the candy might save Christopher's life!

Should he tell them the truth? Racso hesitated. Suddenly he understood *why* Isabella had lied. She had felt hurt by being asked to leave the training unit, and this was a way to make up for that, especially in front of Justin. Isabella wanted to be important and special in the same way he, Racso, had—when, for example, he had lied to the other students about his background. In a way, Isabella was like him. He remembered how her paw had felt when he had grabbed her and pulled her into the thicket above the stream, how she had looked when she was lying there so scared that she couldn't even move. He decided—at least for the time being—to let her have it her way.

But when he got back to the office, only Elvira was there. "Everyone's gone outside," she explained, taking the candy. "Jeremy just arrived! He flew through the storm last night. Finally he couldn't see anymore, so he was forced to hole up in a hollow tree. His feathers are half frozen, so they're building a bonfire to warm him up, and Isabella ran up to the kitchen to make him some soup. But he brought the medicine!"

"That's wonderful!"

Elvira nodded. "He deserves a warm welcome. And our thanks."

"Yes, he does." Dreamily, Racso watched Elvira take a spoonful of the white powder and mix it with water. He couldn't help thinking about the day he and Timothy had arrived at Thorn Valley. He had resented the welcome Timothy got then. And just now he had been arguing with himself about whether to tell the others that he deserved the credit for the candy. In the meantime, Jeremy had been flying through a snowstorm to bring Christopher his medicine—and Jeremy hardly knew Christopher. Maybe Jeremy was really a hero. On the other hand, Nicodemus had said that anyone who tried hard was a hero: "the rat who carries more grain than she really has to, or the student who does not lose his temper when another rat takes what is rightfully his." Racso cringed, remembering the pen. But surely he had redeemed himself. The candy had been hard work, and it had been his idea. . . .

"Racso?"

He started. "I was thinking."

"Christopher drank it all. And he ate two pieces of candy."

"Can I see him?"

Elvira shook her head briskly. "Not yet—he's still very weak. But if he's better tomorrow . . ."

"HOORAY!" Racso felt like dancing around the infirmary. He leaped into the air and cracked his tail backward and forward. "HOORAY!"

"Watch that tail!" Elvira said. "You might knock something over!"

"HOORAY!" Racso couldn't help himself.

Elvira threw her front paws up in the air. "How can I run an infirmary with rats dancing and shouting and waving their tails all over the place?"

"I'm leaving in a minute," Racso said, grinning. "Everyone deserves a chance to celebrate now and then, you know."

"Oh," said Elvira. She looked confused for a moment, but then she smiled. "You're good at it, aren't you?"

"At what?"

"Celebrating."

Now it was Racso's turn to look confused. "Why . . . I suppose I am."

"Maybe one day you'll give me a lesson." Elvira paused, looking thoughtful. She smiled again. "I'd like that," she said.

The Mission

Justin	Beatrice
Arthur	Mitchell
Sally	Vincent
Brendan	Inez
Brutus	Nolan
Timothy	Racso
Fern	

Racso stood in front of the list for a full moment, staring. He closed his eyes and then opened them again. It was still there: Racso. They trusted him. He felt like shouting out loud, but he didn't; after all, there were rats who looked at the list and then walked away quickly, with their heads down. Still he couldn't help puffing out his chest and snapping his tail just slightly as he left the meeting room to look for Timothy.

It was a gray, rainy morning when they left. The last lumps of frozen snow were melting in the steady drizzle, and the ground was soaked.

Nicodemus clasped the paw of each member of the mission. "Good luck," he whispered. "Do the best you can, but be careful. We want you back alive." He smiled. "We'll think about you every day."

When they arrived, the moon was full, and the rats saw that work on the dam had progressed further than they had guessed. The builders had constructed a spillway through the cliff, and most of the water in the river was being diverted through this channel, leaving the riverbed dry enough for work on the base of the dam. Iron pilings had been driven deep into the stony riverbed in two columns, and sheets of thick metal had been placed between these. A narrow walkway had replaced the pontoon bridge. It stretched across the river to the operations center, which sat against the far wall of the cliff like a small concrete house.

The first night Arthur led the others across the

walkway, stopping midway to explain the construction. The rats drew pictures, and measured the structure of the dam in every dimension. By the time they had finished, the sky was beginning to turn gray in the east. They retired to their makeshift office, which was nothing more than a huge bramble in a recess of the cliff about half a mile from the damsite.

Their life was primitive. The bramble was the only space they had found that was big enough to hold all of them at once, so they used it as the headquarters for the mission. They slept in cracks and bushes in the immediate area, either alone or in pairs. For food they gathered anything that grew, sometimes supplementing the roots and acorns with dried seedcakes they had brought from home.

For the first week they did all their explorations together, learning gradually the shape and texture of each facet of the damsite: what it looked like in darkness and moonlight, how it felt to the feet, how it smelled, how far it was from a hole or crack large enough to hide a fleeing rat. There were several lights around the site: one in the lot where the workers and night watchmen parked their cars, and two more on each side of the operations center. These were turned on at five o'clock in the evening and remained on until dawn. The two night watchmen patrolled the site along a regular circuit, varying their route only to stop and smoke a cigarette or drink a soda.

During the day the rats observed a tall man in a business suit and yellow helmet going in and out the door of the operations center. "The chief engineer," Arthur explained. That night he chose Brutus, Sally, and Brendan to help him look the computer over while other rats stood guard outside the door, ready to warn them if the night watchmen should break their routine. The control room was brightly lit, and the computer filled an entire wall. It was a long, narrow machine with a keyboard bordered by dials and gauges. There were three large screens on the wall above the keyboard.

"It's so *big*," Sally whispered. Her heart began to race and her legs trembled. The computer hummed as if it were breathing, and the flickering gauges reminded her of the yellow-green eyes of hawks.

Arthur's voice was reassuring. "The three of you can take cover under this desk while I get my bearings," he said. "Your goal tonight is to memorize the location of everything in the room, so that we can tell the others exactly what to expect. I'm going to look for the computer manual."

Sally wanted to say, "I can't move," but her throat was too dry. And to her surprise, her paws did move when she ordered them to—left, right, left, right—until she was standing beside Brendan and Brutus under the gray metal desk.

They looked around the room. It was messy: Books and papers covered the tables and chairs, and a metal wastebasket was stuffed with trash. A small storeroom to the left of the main room held paint cans, bits of wire screening, cartons of paper, and a stack of plywood. There were metal bookshelves along another wall; near these was a desk with a typewriter on it, and a metal machine with a hinged cover and letters on one side spelling the word "Xerox."

As the others watched, Arthur scanned the bookcase until he found the computer operator's manual. He dragged the book onto an open shelf, and for a while he read. Then he began to take notes. But it seemed as if only minutes had passed before there was a tap on the window—the warning that the night watchman was approaching. Arthur leapt down from the shelf, and all four rats scurried into the storeroom. They found a hiding place under an overturned cardboard box. They held their breath as the heavy boots of the guards walked the length of the control room, coming closer, closer; then, after a pause, the footsteps resumed, walking away. Moments later there were two taps on the window—all clear.

This time Sally climbed up on the shelf with Arthur to help him take notes. He pointed out the word "Jones" scrawled in large letters on the page entitled "Security."

"It's the password into the system," he told Sally. "It means we'll be able to go into the computer and get out any information they've already programmed in."

"Great!" Sally was beginning to feel almost at ease.

Arthur nodded. "But we have a lot of work ahead of us," he said. "This note-taking could wind up being a very slow process."

They continued their work for two nights, entering the operations center after dark, scouting the control room and the adjacent storeroom, taking notes from the operator's manual. Each time a different group went in with Arthur, and he tried to be patient as they exclaimed or trembled or stared wide-eyed when they saw the computer. But he was worried—he needed the information from the manual, so that he could work with it. He needed it now!

It was Racso who realized that there was a faster

way. The word "Xerox" had stuck in his mind for several days, surfacing during odd moments, and while he lay in a dusty crack beside Timothy trying to sleep. Then one evening, just as he was about to bite into his ration of seedcake, he realized what it meant. The hearty male voice from the television commercial popped into his brain. He recited out loud: "The Xerox 223 copier . . . clean, efficient, economical . . . Don't let your office be without one!"

"What?" Beatrice said. "What are you talking about?"

"That's it!" Racso shouted. "A Xerox machine!"

The other rats turned and stared. "What's a Xerox machine?"

"It makes copies on pieces of paper," Racso explained. "We could use it to copy the computer manual. We could probably copy the entire thing in two or three nights."

"Of course," Arthur said. "A copying machine. I've read about them, but I didn't realize what it was."

"Will we be able to operate it?" Vincent asked.

"I'm certain we can figure it out," Arthur said. "Racso and I will go in tonight and try."

And, in fact, using the machine was simple. That night Arthur and Racso copied almost half of the computer manual, handing bunches of the finished copies through the door when they became too bulky and stopping only when they heard the warning tap on the window.

The next night, Racso and Beatrice worked the Xerox machine, leaving Arthur free to analyze the data that had been collected the night before. Vincent and Brutus stood guard outside. The work was slower: for one thing, they ran out of paper, and the carton where they had found more the previous night was now empty. They searched for a full twenty minutes before they found another carton behind the stacks of plywood in the storage room. Then they couldn't decide whether to leave the partially used carton in the space where the empty one had been. They finally arranged the pile so that it looked just as they had found it. So they hurried a little as they copied the final pages of the computer manual and handed the copied sheets out to Brutus to deliver to the runner who was to carry the stack to headquarters.

They struggled to return the heavy manual to its place on the shelf. Racso waited under the desk as Beatrice scurried up on top of the Xerox machine to turn it off for the final time. Her back was to the door when the men came in.

How could it have happened? That was the first thought that flashed through Racso's mind as he saw them, and to his horror they seemed to move in slow motion. Their voices stretched out sleepily into the night: "A RAT! Catch it! *KILL* IT!" One man drew his gun. Beatrice froze in terror.

"Don't fire your gun in here," the other guard said. "You might damage the computer." As he spoke he grabbed the trash can and brought it down over Beatrice's head. "Here, I've got it!"

"Be careful! They can bite, you know."

"I'll put this screening over the top."

Beatrice had come alive now, plunging again and again at the wire cover on the trash can, but Racso could see that it was no use. The guard's gun remained drawn. As soon as they were outside she would be killed. He could not stand the thought, and just as the two men were about to carry their burden out the door, he burst from his hiding place and leaped to the top of the desk. A pencil and paper were lying there. He grabbed the pencil and wrote, in the largest letters he could manage, "STOP!" He held the paper up in front of him with both paws.

Rescue in the Night

"I don't care what we saw," the guard said. "No one will believe us."

The two men were sitting in metal chairs in the office. Almost an hour had passed since they had entered the room to find Beatrice on top of the Xerox machine. Both rats were now imprisoned in the trash can. Three bricks held the screening firm around the top, and the other guard, a balding, heavy man called Hank, was using the trash can as a footrest.

"I mean it, Ray—this is our chance!" he argued. "What do you think Barnum and Bailey would pay for this? Ripley? Even Johnny Carson? A rat who can write! It's got to be worth a million!"

"They wouldn't believe it," Ray answered, rubbing his mustache.

"But we saw it with our own eyes! And we have the sign!"

"Probably it'll never write another word. And when we say it can, they'll think we're nuts."

Hank scratched his head. "Then we'll have to get it to cooperate."

"How?"

"We'll offer it bribes. What do rats like? Cheese? Peanuts? Seeds?"

Ray burst out laughing. "I'll tell you what—if you can get it to write again, I'll go in with you. Otherwise, I say we should stuff them both in a bag with a few bricks and throw them in the river. And then forget it."

Hank wrinkled his brow. "Should I just drop the pencil and paper into the can?"

"Sure, why not?"

Hank did so, making sure that his fingers stayed well above the wire screening. He and Ray peered down at the rats.

Racso looked at Beatrice. She nodded briefly; clearly, if their lives were to be saved, this was the only route. Racso took the pencil in one paw and wrote a brief message. He folded the paper and shoved it to the top of the trash can, where Hank grabbed it.

"Let's see what it wrote!" Ray snatched the paper and read Racso's message out loud: "I am a rat. I like candy."

"What d'you know about that!" Ray exclaimed. He shook his head in astonishment.

"What'd I tell you!" Hank was triumphant. "This is our million, Ray. Our ship has finally come in."

"Give it some candy," Ray said. "Keep it happy!"

Hank fished half a chocolate bar out of his shirt pocket and slid it under the screen. Racso was delighted. He offered a bit to Beatrice, but she shook her head and watched in disbelief as Racso wolfed it down.

"It's almost quarter of five," Ray told Hank. "Why don't we hide them in the storeroom and make one last round? We haven't punched the time clock for three hours—the boss is bound to notice."

Hank felt like saying, "Let him notice!" But he nodded agreeably—why argue now? He hefted the trash can over to a spot behind the stacks of plywood. He laid three boards across the screen, then set three bricks on top of the others. "You guys be good!" he shouted at the rats. "You mean a lot to me!"

*   *   *

Racso and Beatrice heard the door close. They did not speak but let the silence settle into the room once again. They were in absolute darkness. Beatrice's heart was still pounding, and she could feel the blood rushing in her ears. She leaned over to Racso.

"You saved my life," she whispered. "Thank you."

They heard the bricks being moved, one by one, and then the boards. Racso held his breath. Dim light filtered into the trash can, and then the screen came off.

"Are you all right?" Brendan whispered.

"Yes," Racso said. Beatrice did not speak—Racso thought somehow that she could not, at that moment; but she nodded briefly. Justin helped her out of the trash can.

"Quickly," Justin ordered the others, "quickly now." They rolled the trash can back into the office, stacked the boards and bricks neatly in their places, and returned the piece of screening to the shelf.

"What else?" Justin thought out loud. "The notes you wrote, Racso, where are they?"

"Here's one," Arthur answered before Racso could open his mouth. "It was on the desk."

"He put the other one in his pocket when he took the candy bar out," Beatrice said.

"Did the Xerox machine get turned off?"

She nodded. "Right before they came in."

"Okay," Justin said. "Let's get out of here."

They analyzed it later. The primary cause was their own error: Brutus had left his post momentarily to carry the copies to the runner, Nolan; and while Brutus was gone, Vincent had fallen asleep. He awoke just as the men were ascending the ramp to the operations center. By then, there was no way he could tap on the window without being seen. He hoped against hope that they would hear the men from inside and would hide, but the hum of the Xerox machine and the rats' own preoccupation with getting the job done had prevented that. Vincent wrung his paws again and again, although the other rats reassured him: "It could have happened to anyone. And at least we're all safe."

"It proves that we need another guard outside the control room," Brendan said. "That way no one will ever be left alone."

"What about Racso's note?" Timothy asked. "The man had it in his pocket."

"Nobody will believe it," Sally said. "They'll think they're both crazy."

"Or drunk," Arthur said. "I expect they'll be fired if they talk about it."

"What if they can prove they weren't drunk?" Justin asked. He had been silent until this point, and now he was frowning.

"What do you mean?"

"I mean, what if they do convince someone that it really did happen? Not necessarily their bosses— I mean anyone."

"You're kidding, Justin," the others said. "A rat who can read and write?" Brendan winked at Racso.

"But they do have the note. And men convince each other that they've met ghosts and creatures from outer space," Justin argued. "And sometimes they go on TV, or are quoted in the newspapers."

"Then what?" Arthur said. The room had grown silent and was tense.

"There are people who would be interested," Justin said.

The faceless image of Dr. Schultz, the scientist from Nimh, seemed to enter the room. He had traced them to their home under the Fitzgibbons' rosebush years after their escape from the laboratory. Could he still be searching for them?

"The news will never get that far," Arthur said wearily. Then, realizing that he had been arguing with Justin and that both of them were exhausted, he changed his tone. "Anyway, let's hope it won't," he said. "We've got other things to worry about for the next few days."

Arthur was right about that, they all agreed. Almost overnight the icy waters of the Trout had grown warmer, and flowers sprouted on the gray-green cactus plants that grew along the cliff's edge. March rains fell, and the river turned reddish-brown with dirt from the construction site. Now the number of cars that pulled into the parking lot each morning doubled, so that the damsite was like a small city. But in the evenings, it grew still.

One night Racso, Timothy, Brendan, and Sally were assigned to guard duty outside the operations center. It was cold and rainy, and after the security men had come and gone, the four of them met for a moment by the door.

"All clear?" Sally was squad leader for the night.

"All clear."

"We can relax for a moment," Sally said. "The

men are on their way to the trailer to punch in."

Racso was glad. Guard duty was boring. He did a little dance on the wet cement.

Timothy watched with amusement. "What step is that?"

"The hokeypokey." Racso showed off, twirling first one way, then another. Timothy laughed. Racso twirled faster. Then he slipped. He slid across the wet platform, toward the cliff. He grabbed for the guardrail, but it was slippery and he couldn't hold on. He plummeted over the side, into the darkness.

Thoughts flashed like lightning through Racso's mind: *I'm going to die! So this is what my old man was afraid of. I want to scream, but my voice is gone.* That was when he hit the support beam. He grabbed it with all fours and clung there, terrified, until the others lowered a rope and hauled him back up on the platform. He collapsed there in a heap.

"It's okay, Racso. You're going to be okay." That was Brendan's voice. Racso heard Sally calling for reinforcements for guard duty.

Timothy found a piece of burlap in the storeroom and wrapped it around Racso. "Can you walk?" he asked. Racso nodded. "We'll take you back to headquarters."

Racso had to lean on the other three as they made

their way across the walkway, and when they rested on the other side he was still shaking.

"I almost died."

Brendan nodded. "You were lucky to hit that beam."

"I would have been smashed against the rocks." Racso put his face between his paws. He couldn't stop trembling. He thought again of Jenner. He, too, had come close to death. No wonder he was scared—for himself, for Racso, for the whole family. Suddenly Racso longed to tell him that he understood. But he couldn't tell Jenner. He looked at his friends.

"There's something I want to say to you."

Sally was gentle. "Why don't you wait until we get back to headquarters? You'll feel better after you get a chance to rest."

"Now."

They stood looking down at him.

"My father is Jenner," he said. His voice was even, and he was no longer ashamed.

Brendan stared. "Jenner's dead, Racso."

"No more dead than I am," Racso said quietly. And he told them all about it.

*   *   *

They talked for an hour. When they finally got back to headquarters, they discovered that Jeremy had arrived, carrying a flat brown package.

"From Nicodemus," he explained cheerfully. "He's been to the library in Smithville."

They waited until dawn, when all the rats were back, to open it. It contained a wad of newspaper clippings. They came from both local and city papers, and were arranged in chronological order according to when they had been published. Many of them were routine, describing plans for the dam and the proposed lake. Others outlined the controversy with the farmers.

The last articles in the pile described a press conference held by the farmers and a subsequent investigation by a reporter from the *Smithville Tribune*. The rats read these with increasing excitement. Justin volunteered to read the last article out loud. It was headlined "Jones Denies Corruption in Assignment of Dam Contract."

> Yesterday, reporter Lindsey Scott learned that state investigators are trying to find out whether Representative Jones improperly influenced legislation and bidding on the Trout River Dam contract, which was awarded to a company

owned by him and his two cousins. Local farmers charge Jones sponsored the legislation in his
own self-interest. Meanwhile, work at the dam
is continuing at a breakneck pace.

However, farmers charge that the Joneses are
trying to finish the job before a grand jury or-
ders work at the dam stopped.

"YIPPEEEEE!" The rats went wild. They fell on
top of each other trying to read the article for themselves. They laughed and screamed and hugged.

Arthur tried to calm them down. "Much work lies
ahead of us. We don't know whether the farmers
will succeed, and if they do, whether it will be in
time to save the valley. But it's nice to know that
someone else is on our side."

That day, when most of the rats settled into their
separate beds, they slept better than they usually
did, and awoke refreshed.

Operation Sabotage

Nicodemus stretched before he sat down at his desk. The hour was four-thirty in the morning, earlier than he usually got up; but then, most weeks weren't as important as this one, and he needed time to be alone, and to think. Last night, he had turned on the radio. The six-thirty news had *real* news, news that concerned the rats. "Jones Construction Company announced today a grand opening date for the Trout River Dam: Saturday, April eleventh, at twelve noon. The public is invited to attend."

And so it will be sooner than we thought, Nicodemus said to himself. He decided to write to the rats at the damsite to keep them up to date. He got paper, a container of pokeberry ink, and his quill pen from the shelf and laid them on the desk in front of him. He sat quietly for some time, composing the letter in his mind. Then he wrote:

> Our lives have been busy here. My trip to the library was difficult but exciting—I stayed up all night clipping the newspaper articles and skimming the latest editions of *Computer News*. Jeremy flew me home early the next morning.
>
> Yesterday we made our ninth trip to the ridge. We have selected a large dry cave there for an emergency shelter. It has three separate rooms and three entranceways, all of them small enough to keep the foxes out. We have carried three bushels of seeds to the cave, including carrot, cabbage, onion, potato, and tomato seeds. There is a small clearing about 100 yards south where these can be planted. They should produce a crop large enough to feed all of us if we cannot return to Thorn Valley.
>
> We have been observed by other animals and, of course, there have been rumors and panic as the word of the dam has spread to the nests and burrows nearby and farther away. We have tried to reassure those who have come here for information, telling them our plans for an emer-

gency evacuation and urging them to make plans, too.

Christopher continues to recover from his illness. Yesterday Elvira permitted him to leave the nest for the first time since he got sick. He insisted on helping us sort seeds and made a list of all that remained to be carried. He hounds Isabella for the candy recipe and claims that he will carry the mint seeds in his own knapsack.

Listening to the radio last night, I learned that an opening date for the dam has been set: April 11, at noon.

We think of you each day.

The rats at the damsite already knew about the opening date. A banner had been stretched across one end of the parking lot, welcoming the public and picturing the lake with blue water and sandy beaches. Workmen hurried from one part of the site to the next, and trucks rumbled in and out of the parking lot. The concrete walls of the dam glistened in the sunlight. At night the site fell silent once again, belonging only to the night watchmen and the rats.

They had never seen Hank or Ray again. The new watchmen wore uniforms but were no more vigilant than the others. They walked their rounds slowly, stopping often for soda and cigarettes, and punching in on the four time clocks around the site.

Now each evening the couriers brought word of movement throughout the valley. Flying overhead, they could see new paths up the mountainsides, and occasionally they saw caravans of small animals: chipmunks, deer mice, possum. They were leaving, taking nothing but their children. Many of the birds' nests had been deserted, although twice Jeremy had seen songbirds sitting on their eggs or warming young chicks. He had tried to warn them about what was going to happen. But each time they thought he was trying to trick them, and one of the pair would fly at him, shrieking, "GET AWAY! Get away, you horrible crow!"

"But wait," he would shout from above them. "I want to help you! I want to save your lives!"

"You want to eat our children!" the birds would scream.

"Leave the valley!" Jeremy would shout. "Leave the valley, or you will drown!"

Opening day grew nearer: There were five days left, then four, then three. The rats in the mission were scared. They rehearsed their plans: Sally and Timothy, with Racso, Beatrice, and Vincent assisting, would enter the rats' program on the computer the night before the grand opening. Justin would oversee the entire operation. Arthur would stand by to help and would set the fuse for the explosion that would come later. Brutus, Fern, Mitchell, and Nolan would be guards. Brendan and Inez would remain at headquarters in case a courier should arrive with last-minute messages from Thorn Valley.

Arthur was nervous. He reviewed the program with the five rats who were assigned to the computer, giving each of them directions for the appropriate keys. They practiced entering parts of the program one by one. No matter how hard they tried, they made mistakes, and mistakes took time.

One night there was a strange incident, one that Justin attributed to the growing tension in the rats' camp. Three rats were in the operations center, while Brendan, Nolan, and Beatrice stood guard. There was a full moon, so that each of the rats cast a faint shadow as he or she traveled across the dam to the walkway leading to the control room.

Several hours before dawn, Arthur appeared in the doorway and asked Brendan to carry a collection of papers back to headquarters. Brendan scurried away with the load in his knapsack. Beatrice and Nolan could see his shadow as it moved across the pale concrete surface of the dam. After a time the shadow reappeared, but Brendan was nowhere to be seen. Beatrice thought at first that he was playing a trick on them. Then she began to worry. She called softly, but there was no answer. Could he have fallen as he passed from the bridge to the walkway? She remembered the night Racso had slipped on the platform. The waters of the Trout roared hungrily. Beatrice shuddered.

They decided they must tell Justin. Beatrice did so, holding back tears, and she, Justin, and Arthur returned to the walkway to search. There was no sign of him. They were ready to give up hope when Nolan, still standing guard, gave a shout: "There he is!" Sure enough, Brendan came trotting across the walkway straight toward them.

"Where have you *been*?" Justin, Beatrice, and Arthur were so relieved they were not sure whether to laugh or cry.

Brendan looked confused. "Am I late? I stayed at headquarters a little while because a crow had arrived just as I got there. I wanted to make sure there wasn't any urgent news."

"But I saw your shadow on the bridge fifteen minutes ago," Beatrice said.

"It couldn't have been me," Brendan said.

Beatrice's mouth opened, but she snapped it shut.

"Could you have seen the shadow of a bird or a bat?" Arthur's voice was kind.

Beatrice shook her head. "It was one of us."

Nolan, still in the doorway, nodded his head. "I saw it, too."

Arthur touched Beatrice's shoulder. "We're all tired, and we've been under a lot of strain," he said gently.

Beatrice gritted her teeth to keep from yelling at Arthur. How could he presume to know what she had or hadn't seen!

Justin seemed to read her thoughts. "We'll look again," he promised. And before they left for headquarters they spent an hour searching along the dam and the cliffside. They found nothing, and no sign of life. Everyone was puzzled. Beatrice went to bed when they got back to headquarters, but Nolan stayed up, scratching his head, muttering the question that the others had not asked aloud.

"If it was one of us, and it wasn't me, and it wasn't Beatrice, and it wasn't Arthur, and it wasn't Justin, and it wasn't Brendan, then who was it?"

The other rats stared.

"It wasn't *me*," Sally said.

"Or me," said Mitchell.

"Not me, either."

"But who *was* it, then?" Nolan wondered. "Who was it?"

"Twelve o'clock tomorrow," Justin said. "That's when we'll know."

They were standing together on the ridge. It was twilight. The lights at the damsite flicked on. They reminded Timothy of stars wavering in the mist from the river; but there were no stars overhead, no moon; only gray clouds that hung like a dark curtain over the valley and the mountains.

"It's time," Justin said out loud.

They descended from the cliff and hid opposite the concrete runway. The four guards crossed the dam: Brutus, Mitchell, Fern, Nolan. They heard voices before they climbed up the window to look inside the control room, and quickly they lifted both paws: No.

Arthur cursed. "What's the holdup?"

"I don't know." Justin was perplexed, but he stayed calm.

"We've got to get over there and get started!"

"The guards will signal when it's safe. Until then, we'll just have to wait."

And they did wait. A whole hour passed. Arthur and the others were becoming desperate. The plan would fail without enough time! Twice more Brutus appeared on the walkway and raised both paws in the signal that meant no. Then suddenly the door to the control room opened, and two people came out. One, a man, wore a yellow helmet and carried a briefcase. The other was a young woman, with red hair and glasses. She carried a notepad, and even as she crossed the bridge she asked questions. As they strolled closer, some of the man's words were audible: "All set . . . big success . . . ready to roll." The rats watched silently as the two humans walked to the parking lot, where they got into separate cars and drove away. At the same moment Brutus appeared on the walkway and gave the signal: all clear.

The rats scurried across the dam and took their assigned positions in the control room: Sally and Timothy at the computer keyboard, Arthur beside the file drawers, Racso, Beatrice, and Vincent under the metal desk waiting to be called on. Justin stood on top of the desk, where he could see everyone. He checked the wall clock: 10:26. He gave the order to proceed.

The master disks for the humans' computer programs were stored in a long, narrow drawer marked "Trout River Dam System." Arthur opened it and handed the first disk to Racso, who inserted it in the computer. The screen lit up with the shimmering pattern of titles all the rats knew by now: "Metrosystems Inc. Trout River Dam Operational System: Units I, II, III, IV." Timothy typed in the password and pushed the button marked "Erase."

Justin kept the time. Everything they did, they did fast, and there were few mistakes. Yet they were behind. Precious time had been lost during the reporter's visit. They struggled to catch up.

By midnight the master disks had been erased. Now Vincent spread Arthur's program beside the keyboard. The rats knew it well; they had practiced it night after night, but they had never completed the program in fewer than eight hours. Now there were only six. Racso inserted one of the blank disks and Timothy typed the password, "Jones." He and Sally began to enter the program. No one spoke. Vincent added new pages one by one as keys flashed under gray paws. Timothy's mind filled with images as he worked: the valley, Emerald Pond, the classroom at Thorn Valley. He thought of his mother, snug in the cinder-block house in Mr. Fitzgibbon's field. This is for her, he thought; this is for Cynthia, this is for Martin, this is for Teresa. And his paws moved faster.

The numbers made him dizzy. He typed them

anyway, trying to appreciate Arthur's genius in fig-
uring them out. He had known at one time what
each number represented—the depth of the water
in the lake, the pressure of the water on each square
inch of the concrete dam, the tons of water released
when a spillway rose one foot for a period of ten
minutes. But that was too much to think about right
now. Instead, he made up a song in his mind, to
match the rhythm of his paws: I hope it works, I
hope it works, I hope it works.

Twice, at the expected time, Brutus tapped on
the window to warn that the security patrol was
coming. Then, of course, the disk was removed, the
papers hidden, the computer turned off. The rats
and Timothy crouched in a dark corner of the storage
room. Each time the night watchmen strolled through
the room, they noticed nothing.

Three o'clock came. Arthur unbolted a section in
the side of the computer and wriggled in, carrying
his supplies with him. He had measured his fuses
carefully, knowing that it would be no victory if the
explosion came too soon; after all, the computer was
replaceable. But for both the dam and the computer
to be destroyed! He whistled under his breath to
keep calm.

From his perch on the metal table, Justin saw the

clock reach four. He looked toward Vincent, holding the sheaf of papers still to be placed one by one beside the computer keyboard. Beatrice had removed the finished pages to a stack under the desk. The stack was thick, but not thick enough; a full third of the program remained. Justin's throat felt dry. He looked out the window. Was there a faint gray streak in the east already? He looked again at the clock on the wall: four-thirty.

Sally was exhausted. She gasped and threw her head to one side as if she were about to faint. Racso helped her down from the keyboard, and Beatrice took her place.

Faster, faster! Beatrice typed the numbers from the program as if she were running in place. Then she looked at the viewing screen and saw that she had made a mistake. She had put the decimal point in the wrong place for every number in the whole column! Slowly, painstakingly, she corrected each error. A tear splashed down the gray fur of her cheek.

Arthur came out of the computer. He looked first at the clock. The time was four forty-five. By sunrise they must be gone. He looked at the papers in Vincent's arms. He shook his head and looked at Justin.

He climbed the gray table wearily and stood beside him.

"This is it, isn't it?" His voice was barely audible.

Justin's whiskers drooped, and his eyes looked sad and tired.

"You mustn't blame yourself," he said. "We knew there would be factors beyond our control. We couldn't predict the interview."

"Timing," Arthur muttered. He watched the second hand of the clock advance one full cycle, then another. If only they could stop it or slow it down! But even then, the earth would not slow its orbit. No matter what the clock said, the sunlight would be there in the east. Sunrise. He swallowed hard.

Justin called the others to him. The clock read five.

"We must save ourselves," he said.

They argued.

"In another half hour we might be done. We have to try. We have to!"

"We would be found," Justin said.

"No!" Sally said. She was crying.

"We must leave now," Justin said evenly. He sounded hoarse. He gestured to Racso to pick up the loose pages of the computer program and to turn off the computer. Racso did this, feeling a great weight. He could hardly bear to look at the other rats.

They were standing together at the door, preparing to leave, when something happened. The lights went out.

Hero Without a Name

"A power failure!"

They looked at each other in astonishment. Behind them, for the first time they could remember, the room was completely silent. Somewhere, in a narrow rocky passageway in the mountain, its lifeline—an electric cable—had been cut. Deliberately, methodically, someone else had plotted to destroy the dam.

Justin, of course, did not know this; nor did any of the rats perched so solemnly in the doorway of the operations center. They were certain of only one thing: their own failure. They paused and looked up the valley: the rugged cliffs, the river, the silhouette of earth and sky. They felt sadness and longing.

Arthur, ever practical, broke the silence. "Look— the power's out all over the site, even in the parking lot! They'll have to use the emergency generators."

Sure enough, the long asphalt rectangle just below the road through the mountain pass was dark. But even as they stood looking, a pair of headlights appeared over the black rim of the pass. The humans were on their way to work.

"Let's get out of here!" Justin's voice was like a whip cracking. "Quickly!"

Inside headquarters, the others stood around in stony silence as Arthur argued with Sally.

"They're safe in the cave at the top of the ridge. They went there last night. They don't expect to hear from us until we can send them a full report— and that includes an investigation of the blackout."

"They should know the worst." Sally stamped her hind foot. "You just don't want to give up, to admit that we've failed!"

"We're not certain that we *have* failed!" Arthur snapped. "I don't think they can open the damsite without electricity."

"You know as well as I do that they have emergency generators."

"But those are a backup system. They can only supply a limited amount of power."

Sally's teeth clenched in anger. "The rest of us want to go home," she hissed. "This is a time when all of us should be together!"

"All I want is a few hours!" Arthur shouted. "A few hours, to find out what went wrong!"

Racso watched quietly. He had never seen the rats like this. Rats at home argued and hissed when they fought over a dainty morsel or a nest closer to the warmth of the steam pipes. But the rats of Thorn Valley were reasonable, cooperative, well-mannered. He turned toward Justin, but Justin was sitting alone in the corner, looking tired and dazed. Then he caught Beatrice's eye. She stepped forward and held her paws up between Arthur and Sally. She spoke softly.

"We're all tired, and that makes it easier to fly off the handle. Sally, you and Arthur worked terribly hard last night, and you both did a good job. The rest of us did, too. We need rest. If Arthur wants to go out and investigate while we're sleeping, let him. Perhaps he'll find that we can take advantage of the blackout. And if that's true, we must do so."

The rats nodded, except for Sally, who looked away. Arthur looked relieved.

Suddenly, Timothy felt a surge of interest. "I want to go, too."

"Me, too," Racso said.

"Sure," Arthur said, "come along."

From their hiding place on the cliffside, Arthur, Timothy, and Racso watched the first efforts to restore the electrical system. Within minutes the workmen realized that the cable had broken somewhere inside the foot-wide tunnel that funneled the electric main through the mountainside. They turned their attention to the emergency generators in the basement of the operations center. When these failed to start, they grew frantic. A cry spread across the damsite. Racso strained his ears to hear. The word the men were shouting was "Sabotage!"

Timothy hurried back to headquarters and woke the others, and soon they were stretched out on a narrow ledge above the site. Their voices were hushed with excitement.

"Who besides us?" Justin whispered. "Who besides us would care?"

"The farmers," Timothy answered readily.

"Or the man in the canoe," Racso said. "He cared about the valley. He thought it was beautiful and shouldn't be destroyed."

"But we would have seen them!"

"The farmers *are* here," Justin interrupted. A crowd had begun to gather for the grand opening, and beyond them, on the edge of the parking lot, a line of men and women were marching with banners. Timothy's sharp eyes could make out the biggest words: "SAVE OUR FARMS!" He was surprised to see Mr. and Mrs. Fitzgibbon walking side by side. Mr. Fitzgibbon was wearing a suit and looked terribly out of place. Suddenly, in the midst of all the excitement, Timothy felt homesick, and longed to see his family and the cinder-block house in the garden.

The crowd got bigger. Out of the operations center came the chief engineer. His yellow hat was a bright dot in the late-morning sunlight. The rats saw his mouth opening and closing, saw him stamp his foot on the cement. Three men in business suits rushed up, shouting and waving their arms.

[252]

"The Joneses themselves, I believe," Justin said as if he had made the introductions personally. "And they do seem a bit upset."

"There won't be any grand opening today," Arthur said, grinning. "It will take at least a day to fix the cable and the generators."

"Giving us another night to work on our program?"

Justin smiled a big smile. "All the time we'll need, I should think."

By noon, the parking lot was packed with people. They shouted and clapped. Nothing happened. At one o'clock, when Representative Jones stood up to make a speech, they were still clapping. He had a microphone, but because there was no electricity, it didn't work, so he looked to the rats on the ledge above him like a little puppet whose mouth opened and closed wordlessly. Photographers gathered around, taking his picture. But as the word spread through the crowd that there would be no grand opening, a roar of protest began. "BOOOOOOO-OOOOOOOO!" shouted the people. Someone threw a paper cup and hit him on the leg. Then a young boy threw a hard-boiled egg that just missed his shoulder. The police came and surrounded Representative Jones, and shouted through megaphones that the crowd must go home.

The rats stayed in their hiding place on the ledge until the people were gone. That afternoon they watched as workmen placed long silver ladders against the cliff and climbed up until they were only a hundred feet below the spot where the rats lay. The same reporter they had seen the night before stood below the workmen and watched as they pulled the broken cable from the tunnel. As they did so, something slid out of the opening and fell to the ground below. What was it? The rats strained to see.

"It's an animal," the reporter shouted. "Whatever it is, it's badly burned."

"Whatever it was, you mean."

She didn't laugh. They saw her bending over the small dark object. She said, "It smells awful."

"It must have been in the tunnel when the cable shorted out," one of the workmen said. "It was probably looking for food and bit through the rubber insulation."

"It's the culprit, all right," the other workman added. "You can see the tooth marks here on the wire."

"Jones thought it was sabotage, when both the cable and the generators went out at once. He thought the farmers did it."

The first man laughed. "Whoever wrecked those generators knew what he was doing," he said. "But anyone with a brain would have known that to break the rubber on that cable was certain death."

"Of course he knew," Justin said later. The rats were in their headquarters. They were numb.

"But who?" Arthur asked. "And why?"

"I don't know. But he gave us a chance to complete our mission."

"He died to save the valley," Sally said quietly.

Timothy frowned. "Could he have known about us?"

Beatrice answered quickly, softly. "I believe he did. I believe we glimpsed him on the ramp that night. He was on his way to sabotage the generators. He hid, but he must have heard us searching."

Justin nodded. "He didn't come out. He had his own plan, and he intended to carry it out."

"We must find out who he was," Arthur said. "He has a family somewhere, and they must be told that he's dead, and how brave he was."

* * *

They agreed to go to sleep, and they slept that night and part of the following morning. When they awoke, there was still no electricity at the site. Since they couldn't complete the mission until the cable was repaired, the rats agreed to search for clues to the identity of the stranger. They decided to look for anything: a paper, a scrap of cloth, a bit of left-over food. They searched along the ridge in each direction, looking in every bush and crack, but they found nothing.

It was Timothy who realized there was some-where else to look.

"He could climb!" he said suddenly. "He climbed up and down the canyon wall to get to the tunnel where the cable comes through. And the cliff there is almost sheer."

"There are small caves in the cliff," Justin said slowly. "But it would be dangerous to search them. We have no ropes."

"If we are careful, I think we can inch our way down the rock," Timothy said.

Justin shook his head. "Too risky."

"I know where there's some rope!" Brendan spoke up.

"Can you get it without being seen?"

Brendan nodded. "I'm sure I can."

"Good. We'll start as soon as you get back."

Timothy and Justin went first. They descended the cliff slowly, searching the dark rock for footholds. It took them about a half hour to reach the first cave. It was empty.

They climbed north along the wall, toward the site. They made slow progress, for the ropes became tangled, and they had to climb up the rocks to pull them free. After a time, they stopped on a shelf of rock to rest.

"It's a hard climb," Timothy said.

Justin nodded. "Some rats are more used to scaling steep walls than we are," he said. "My mother grew up climbing in and out the window of a storeroom on the fifth floor of an apartment building. She could get over a brick wall as easily as you or I can write our names." His face grew sad. "I don't even know whether she's alive now," he said. "We lost touch with each other during the time I was at Nimh, and I haven't been home since."

"Thorn Valley's your home now," Timothy said.

Justin nodded. "Or wherever the colony ends up."

"Yes." For the second time in two days Timothy

was homesick. Briefly, he imagined his mother gathering peanuts from the back field for their supper, Martin laughing, Cynthia and Teresa splashing each other amid the clear ripples of the brook.

"We should go on," Justin said. "It will soon be sunset."

His camp was in the third cave. He had left his possessions in a neat pile, as if he'd hoped they would be found. There was a dingy rag—his bed—neatly folded and, beside this, a small gray knapsack.

Justin opened it. He found two pieces of chocolate fastened together with string. Under the string was a note. It read simply, "For O." And in the bottom of the knapsack was a scrap of newspaper. It was deeply creased, as if it had been folded and refolded many times. Timothy opened it and saw a map of Thorn Valley. Over this was the headline, "State Forest to Become Lake." There was an article describing the dam and the plan to flood the valley. Someone had drawn an arrow from the map to the margin of the paper. Beside it was written a message. Timothy held the paper up to catch the last strong rays of the setting sun. He made out the words along the margin, one by one:

My son
is
here.
He
can-
not
swim.

It was nearly dark when Justin and Timothy got back to headquarters. They carried with them the gray knapsack. Timothy asked to be left alone with Racso, and he showed Racso what they had found.

When Racso first saw the knapsack he felt as if he were seeing a ghost. It had hung on a nail beside the sewer pipe for as long as he could remember. His mother had worn it when she went out to gather food for the family; Racso had loved to empty it for her and hang it back on the nail again. Timothy showed him the chocolate, too, and the newspaper clipping, but Racso just shook his head stubbornly.

"He never went out, not after the accident. He was afraid to leave the nest. He didn't even want us to leave, because he was afraid of what might happen to us."

Timothy listened without speaking.

"There's no way he could have come this far. It's all a mistake." Racso glanced desperately at the paper, the candy, the knapsack. "Isn't it, Timothy?" His voice was pleading.

Timothy didn't answer. Instead, he picked up the little packet of chocolate. "For O," he read softly. "O, for Oscar."

"NO!" Racso began to cry. He pictured Jenner's face: scarred, lonely, frightened. Racso had run away, but Jenner had come after him.

"I want him back," Racso sobbed.

Timothy put one paw on Racso's shoulder.

Then Racso lost control of himself. The discipline and restraint he had learned at Thorn Valley slipped away, and he was a little child again. He lay down on the ground and pounded his paws against the dirt. He screamed, "I WANT MY FATHER!"

Timothy stayed with Racso through the night. There was no need to explain what had happened; when Justin told the group about the note, Brendan and Sally realized at once that Jenner had written it. With Racso's permission they told the others what they knew. Everyone was astonished. They were also sorry for Racso, and they did what they could to make him feel better. Brutus and Nolan made him a bed out of shredded papers, and Beatrice cooked a little pot of mushroom tea for him. Timothy put him to bed. Racso was exhausted from crying. Within minutes his eyelids drooped, and his breathing became peaceful and still.

In the morning, before Racso was awake, Justin came in and sat down beside Timothy.

"Arthur and I stayed up talking last night," he whispered. "We've decided to leave Arthur, Sally, Brutus, and Beatrice here to finish programming the computer—Arthur thinks it can be done tonight. The rest of us will go home. There will be a lot of people on the site today. It will be safer to have most of us gone."

Justin paused, and then he sighed wearily. "Jeremy is due in this morning," he continued. "He'll be flying back to Mr. Fitzgibbon's farm after he makes his delivery. I'm going to ask him to take you with him. You must tell Mrs. Frisby and the others what has happened, and what we expect to happen. We'll send a message as soon as the job is done."

Timothy nodded. He knew that he should volunteer to stay on to help Arthur and the others, but at the same time he felt tired, more tired than he had ever been in his whole life. More than anything he wanted to go to sleep in his own bed, to wake up to the rippling of the brook and the faraway hum of Mr. Fitzgibbon's tractor as it turned the soil for the planting of the summer crops.

Justin seemed to know what he was thinking. "It's been a hard year for you."

"Exciting, too." Timothy looked at Racso, curled up on the bed. It seemed as if they had known each other forever. Their friendship was a fact now, as solid as the heavy walnuts that dropped from the branches of the gnarled tree beside the creek each September, as reliable as the thawing of frozen fields in spring.

Justin followed Timothy's gaze. "We'll take good care of him."

"I know. It's just that I'm not sure I should leave so soon."

Justin was firm. "Jenner left him with us. He trusted us to raise him. We can help him through this. And he'll be there in the fall, when you come back to school." Justin paused. "Your family is waiting to see you."

Timothy closed his eyes and smiled. He imagined a celebration of his homecoming, a special dinner of fresh peas and cauliflower and mushrooms. He imagined getting the message that the dam was destroyed and the plans for the lake abandoned. It was hard to open his eyes again, to see the bleak walls of the headquarters and Justin's lined face.

"Yes," he said slowly, "I'm ready to go home."

In Memoriam

The newspaper told the story, adding headline after
headline until it seemed that the whole world had
nothing to talk about except the scandal of the Trout
River Dam. The rats posted the articles along the
wall of the meeting room.

Blackout Blocks Opening of
Trout River Dam

Gate Malfunction
Damages T. R. Dam

More Trouble at Thorn Valley:
Dynamite Destroys Computer

State Nixes Funds in Jones Scandal
Jones: "It Was Sabotage!"

There was another article, too, clipped from the back pages of the *Smithville Tribune*. Its headline was "Rumor Ties Rats to Dam Problems," and it was written by Lindsey Scott. The story included interviews with two night watchmen who claimed to have met an intelligent rat in the computer operations center one night and who had subsequently been fired; and with a workman who had reason to believe that a rat had actually severed the electric cable that powered the dam. A third source claimed to have seen the black, oily tracks of a small mammal outside the entrance to the emergency generator system. Although Representative Jones refused to make any specific charges concerning the rats, he was quoted as saying that the farmers would stop at nothing to close the dam. A spokesman for the farmers said simply, "We thank God for what happened, and if there were others involved, we thank them, too."

Most of the rats found the article amusing, but Justin felt uneasy about it. He wondered what Lindsey Scott had thought as she interviewed the workmen. The article didn't suggest that they were crazy, or even drunk. Would she guess that there were rats who lived in Thorn Valley and wanted it preserved? Would she remember the place along the creek where she had found the little basket and try to return there? Would she begin to wonder how rats could become so smart that they could read and write, or even program a computer? Would she talk to scientists? He shuddered. Perhaps his imagination was running away with him. He wanted to think so, but he couldn't be sure.

Most of the rats concluded that their problems with the dam were over. They celebrated by spending long afternoons swimming and splashing in Emerald Pond or lying on the banks eating juicy wild strawberries. Their relief turned to laughter. The younger rats built a diving platform out of stones and bamboo, and performed acrobatic feats as they leaped from it into the cool water. Under the cautious coaching of Christopher and Brendan, Racso learned to swim. He was extremely proud of himself as he paddled from one edge of the pond to the other, and he was apt to flick his tail across the surface of the water to splash Isabella, who responded with indignant squeals.

Her attitude toward Racso had changed. As a member of the successful sabotage unit, he was admired by everyone. And it had been his father—Jenner—who had given his life to stop the dam. Not only that, but Justin had announced his intention of getting married—to someone else! There had been a whole week when Isabella felt like growling each time she heard the name "Beatrice." She told Justin how she felt, and he was gentle and kind, but he didn't say anything about changing his plans. Finally Isabella just gave up. If Justin didn't appreciate her, maybe somewhere there was a rat who did! She remembered how Racso had let her take credit for saving Christopher. Maybe being short wasn't so bad after all! The next time Isabella saw Racso, she took off her dirty apron and twirled her whiskers around one paw to make them curl. The following day she made up a big batch of peppermint candy and left it outside the door to his bedroom. Racso ate it all at one sitting. He got sick, and Isabella brought him soup and wiped his forehead with a wet rag.

It was Beatrice who suggested that a special stone be erected in honor of Jenner, who had helped save Thorn Valley. She talked with Hermione, Justin, and Nicodemus, and they agreed to hold a memorial service for him in the fall, after the stone was carved and set in place.

*   *   *

When another letter arrived in the Fitzgibbons' south field—dropped by courier crow among the cabbages and black-eyed peas—the animals who found it guessed at once whom it was for. They had all heard about Timothy's role in saving their homes. They also knew of Mrs. Frisby's bravery in flying all the way to Thorn Valley to warn the rats about the dam. Although they could not read the neatly lettered envelope, they hurried together—a chipmunk, two moles, and the shrew—to the Frisbys' summer house beside the brook.

"It's for you!" they chorused when Mrs. Frisby appeared in the doorway. "A crow dropped it just ten minutes ago! We saw it fall and brought it right away!"

"Open it at once!" the shrew commanded, as if the letter were her own.

But Mrs. Frisby was flustered. She could not help but remember the first letter, which had brought the news about Timothy. These past months had been so wonderful, with her family all together and the threat of the dam gone, that she really did not want to open the letter. What if it held bad news? Then she saw it was addressed not just to her, but also to Timothy. She called him from the bedroom, where he had been busy polishing his rock collection.

"What is it, Mother?"

"We have—"

"You got a letter, and we found it in the garden—we saw the crow drop it, and we knew it was for you, so we brought it right away," the shrew interrupted in a bossy voice. "It's from the rats, I'm sure!" She smiled at Timothy, and her voice grew softer. Like all the other animals on the farm, she regarded him as a hero. "Open it, Timothy!"

Timothy carefully slit the birch-bark envelope and pulled out a sheet of paper. The borders were decorated with pokeberry ink, and in the center of the page there was a printed invitation, which Timothy read out loud.

A Memorial Service
for Jenner
will be held at Thorn Valley
September 10 at 10:00 A.M.

Under the invitation was a note in wobbly handwriting: "I hope you can come. We have invited Jeremy, too. Love, Racso."

Timothy looked eagerly at his mother. "Can I go? Can I, Mother?"

Mrs. Frisby hesitated, but only for a moment. "You will need to get to school anyway," she said. "And I would certainly rather have you fly than walk by yourself!"

"But what about you, Mrs. Frisby?" the shrew asked. "*You* are invited, too."

Mrs. Frisby smiled. "But I am needed here at home, with Cynthia and Teresa. And anyway, I don't really deserve to be there. My part in this adventure was a small one."

"I will watch Cynthia and Teresa," the shrew announced, "because *you* must go. You flew there before, to tell them about the dam—that was an act of courage. And now you must fly there to thank them, for all of us."

Mrs. Frisby looked at the shrew with some surprise. It was not like her to offer expressions of gratitude. The chipmunk and the moles, usually shy and retiring, nodded their heads in agreement and looked intently at Mrs. Frisby.

"Well," she said, half to herself, "I hadn't thought of it that way. . . ."

"Do come, Mother," Timothy said. "Your last visit was so short, you didn't even get to see our playground."

Mrs. Frisby smiled. It would be nice to visit Thorn

Valley without feeling worried, to relax and talk with her friends Justin and Nicodemus. "Well," she said softly. "Perhaps I will."

There were no strangers among the group that gathered in the pine grove on that special September day. Racso was delighted to see Timothy, who would be staying at Thorn Valley to go to school. They reminded each other that it had been almost exactly a year since the day they had met. They laughed about that autumn afternoon when Timothy had tasted candy for the first time and Racso had met a field mouse who could read.

The stone itself was beautiful, a white quartz about five inches tall. The rats had engraved it with the name "Jenner" in a flowing script, and beneath this, at Racso's request, the word "hero." The stone was set into the cool green moss along the bank of the brook, close to the memorial marked "R."

The ceremony consisted of two speeches, with a break in between for refreshments. Beatrice gave the first speech. She talked about a moonlit night in a place where most of the rats had never been. She talked about a shadow so quick and faint that she and Nolan had to reassure themselves they had seen it at all.

"We were the last ones to see him alive," she said. "We didn't even see his face. If we had, I don't think we would have believed it, because to most of us, Jenner was already dead. But we had forgotton that Jenner was a rebel. The accident in the hardware store killed six others, but it didn't kill him. With incredible willpower, he saved himself."

Beatrice paused. "We can only guess what it must have been like for him, to leave the nest again after three years, but we *can* guess this: that he feared more for Racso than he did for himself. He developed a plan to stop the dam, and that plan became his world. That night on the ramp, we called out to him, but he didn't answer. He may not have known who we were, or that Racso was with us. Or he may have known, and feared that we would destroy his plan. He may have guessed that we would fail but was certain that he would not.

"The terrible days of the mission are ended, and are like a dream for us now," Beatrice said. "But the deeds of Jenner will live on. He has taken his place in our history, and among our heroes."

Beatrice walked over and stood beside the monument. She touched it with one paw. She looked into the faces of the rats in front of her. "To you, Jenner, father of Racso, I dedicate this stone," she said. "Though time will pass, you will never be forgotten."

There was a moment of silence. Tears streamed from Racso's eyes, and he made no motion to wipe them away. Other rats cried, too. Still others sat quietly, thinking of the adventures that had befallen them since their escape from the laboratory years ago. Mrs. Frisby thought of her husband, Jonathan, who had given his life trying to secure the future of the colony. She felt shy, but proud. She knew that Timothy had returned to the farm from the sabotage mission tired, but different: There was a self-confidence about him that she had never seen before. Watching him sitting in the moss between Racso and Isabella, she realized that he had grown up.

But it was only an instant later that Timothy snatched Racso's hat. He waved it once and headed straight for the brook.

"Hey, give that back!" Racso grinned and shook his paw. "That's my hat!"

"Come and get it!"

"I'll get it—don't you worry, Racso!" Christopher raced for the water. He looked lithe and strong; it was hard for Mrs. Frisby to imagine that he had been so sick only months before. Elvira had done her job well—although there had been help from others, of course. Christopher did a swan dive off the bank and swam after Timothy, who had the hat between his teeth.

"YOU'D BETTER GIVE THAT BACK!" Isabella stood on her hind legs on the bank, squealing. "RACSO NEEDS THAT!"

"Does he, now?" Brendan gave a hard push and Isabella was wet up to her neck. He jumped in behind her. "Racso, I adore you," he cooed. "You mad hatter of a scientist! You loving laboratory worker! You peppermint king!"

"You'll be sorry, Brendan!" But when Isabella saw that even Racso was laughing, she laughed, too. Timothy threw her the hat, and she put it on. She looked at her reflection in the water, shook her head, and threw the hat back to Racso, who plopped it, sopping, on his own head.

The young rats played in the brook until the refreshments were served: nut cakes and wild grape juice. The older rats chatted. Those who were strangers introduced themselves to Mrs. Frisby. She met Elvira, the doctor, and Bertha, the gardener. She met Hermione and Nolan and Beatrice. She talked with Justin and Arthur, who had helped to move her house years before.

Mrs. Frisby was a bit startled to see that the fur around Nicodemus's nose had turned white. He was growing old! She remembered that the rats had thought that shots they had received in the laboratory at Nimh would keep them young forever. So they had been wrong. She sighed. She did not like to think of a world without Nicodemus in it.

But a cheerful voice interrupted her mood.

"Turn around, everyone! Look at Jeremy!"

Mrs. Frisby scurried around the larger rats just in time to see Justin fasten a medal around Jeremy's neck. The medal was round, with a large, glittery "J" in the middle.

"For your part in the sabotage mission we wish to honor and thank you with this medal," Justin said. "It was made especially for you by Racso and Christopher."

"It's shiny!"

"It's made from chips of mica," Racso explained. "We glued it on by ourselves."

"Thank you!" In his delight, Jeremy hopped from one foot to the other. He flapped his wings. "I'm going to fly home and show it to my friends!"

"Don't leave without Mrs. Frisby," Nicodemus said. "She's counting on you for a ride."

"I forgot all about her." Jeremy hung his head, but a second later Sally appeared with a basket of wild figs.

"Aren't these your favorites? We saved them for you."

Jeremy's eyes gleamed. He swallowed the figs whole, one after another.

Nicodemus made the closing speech. He talked about the bonds between rats: the web of parents and grandparents and great-grandparents going so far back in time that some claimed that all rats were descended from just one family. He talked about Jenner's love for Racso, which had caused him to give up his own life to save his son.

"For some, love is the strongest force there is," Nicodemus said. "Rats like these—Martha and Red and Jenner—are the most likely to risk their lives for others, and to become heroes. In doing so, they show a greatness of spirit that is wonderful and moving to think of.

"I myself have never been like that," Nicodemus said, somewhat sadly. "My mind has been more inclined to the practical, to the tasks at hand: the planting of seeds, the teaching of our children, the building of our home. And my goals for the colony have been practical ones: cooperation, efficiency, organization. Yet these alone were not enough to stop the dam."

Nicodemus paused. He looked directly at Racso. "You told me once that you dreamed of becoming a hero," he said. "I remember I told you that we did not breed heroes here, and that everyone must do his part in making the community strong."

Nicodemus smiled. "I still believe that," he said. "But if young rats should find their minds wandering sometimes to heroic feats, or if they dream of triumphs and victories we have not yet undertaken to win, I wish them well. And if I should see them here in the pine grove, sitting alone beside these monuments, I will bide my time before I send them back to work or school."

Evening fell on Thorn Valley. The sun, a glowing ball against the dark stone of the mountain, cast a reddish light over the brambles and woodlands. Most of the rats had already gone indoors when Mrs. Frisby kissed Timothy good-bye and climbed up Jeremy's wing to sit behind his head. They rose in the sky and circled once. Usually, Mrs. Frisby kept her eyes shut tight while she was flying, but for some reason she opened them as they completed the wide circle. She looked down. Far beneath them she could see the dark shapes of Timothy and three rats, sitting together beside the brook. Their heads were close together, as if they were deep in conversation. Although she could not identify the rats, she could see that one was shorter than the rest.

Then Timothy looked up and saw Jeremy. By now, he was so high up that his body was only a black spot against the broad expanse of the evening sky. Although he was sure that the crow couldn't see him, he raised his paw and waved it once, twice, three times. Jeremy seemed to hover in one spot, and for an instant Timothy imagined that he could see his mother on the crow's back, looking down at him. Then the bird flew higher, and within a minute, they were gone.